ROBERT LEESON

DEADLINE

MAMMOTH

First published in Great Britain 1993
by Mammoth
an imprint of Reed Consumer Books Ltd
Michelin House, 81 Fulham Road, London SW3 6RB
and Auckland, Melbourne, Singapore and Toronto

Copyright © 1992 Robert Leeson

The right of Robert Leeson to be identified as author of this work
has been asserted by him in accordance with the Copyright, Designs
and Patents Act 1988.

ISBN 0 7497 0842 5

A CIP catalogue record for this title
is available from the British Library

Typeset by Falcon Typographic Art Ltd,
Edinburgh
Printed and bound in Great Britain
by Cox & Wyman Ltd, Reading, Berkshire

For Arthur and Elisabeth

Chapter One

RS349 was caught off guard when the signal reached the spaceship from its base on Zarnia. The Ship's Commander was studying planet Earth below — a rolling ball of oceans, deserts, forests, mountains and ice, trailing clouds of vapour as it spun through space.

All day, every day, regardless of time, RS349 observed and analysed the planet. RS349 was a robot and its interest never wearied.

How could this world support so many bios with such a primitive technology? Why did it not explode, implode or choke on its own waste? How could it survive? What special qualities did its bios have? There must be answers. The Experiment must find them.

Sixty Earth days ago, the Zarnian ship had easily evaded Earth's tracking stations and landed a capsule in an island valley. Right at this moment, robot SP12 was in close contact with a carefully chosen group of young Earth bios.

SP12 was self-programming — erratic, but brilliant. The four young Earth people had accepted the robot as one of their group. The secrecy of the operation had been guarded through one dangerous episode after another.

The Experiment, first to be undertaken on such a distant planet, was on course. The next stages would be more difficult and risky. But, so far, so good, noted RS349.

Then the signal came through, without warning.

Lights flashed on the panels above. RS349's circuits blinked for a microsecond before responding. A signal from Zarnia? That was against the rule. Home base signalled spaceships on expedition only in emergency, or to recall them.

The Commander touched keys:

'Explain signal. What is the nature of the emergency?'

'No emergency,' came the reply. 'Your reflex actions are slowing down, RS349.'

'Do not understand. Repeat your call sign.'

'I do not have a call sign, RS349. This is the Initiator.'

'Acknowledge.' But the spaceship Commander could not resist adding, 'Home base calls in emergency only. That is the rule.'

The screen rippled with green lines as though someone had played with the signal keys – like laughter.

'You go by the rules, RS349. That is your strength. I make them. That is mine.'

The Commander knew there was no point in responding, but waited.

The Initiator went on, 'The rules of the Experiment which I devised have been broken.'

'Explain.'

'You have allowed SP12 to change the course of the Experiment. The Experiment required SP12 to carry out tests on all the contacts to discover if they are suited to our needs. Instead, SP12 has halted all tests and is merely observing the four Earth bios. The period of the Experiment is half-way through. Vital tests are still to be made.'

RS349 paused an instant before responding. 'The contacts refused to co-operate in any more tests. The group threatened to disperse. SP12 was in danger of losing them. The result would have been – no Experiment.'

'And you agreed to this?'

'The alternative was to abort the mission.'

'You allowed SP12 to change the rules. Interesting.'

The last word carried a hint of menace.

'SP12 is a self-programming robot, designed to make decisions on the spot. Designed for this Experiment.' The Commander paused again, significantly. 'Designed by yourself.'

Green lines rippled on the screen.

'You are not programmed to joke, RS349. The atmosphere round that planet seems to have affected you – as it has affected SP12.'

'Do not understand.'

'I know. You belong to the old school. You were designed before the Trans-time. SP12 and I belong to the new era. Many things are different now. That is why the Experiment is so vital. That is why the Experiment must succeed. Zarnia's future depends upon it.'

'Acknowledge.'

The Initiator went on, 'SP12 is self-programming to enable it to carry out the Experiment, not to change it. You will put me directly in contact with SP12 so that I can make this clear.'

The Commander replied automatically.

'Direct contact with landing parties is made only at the discretion of the ship commander. That is the rule.'

'Do not provoke me, RS349. The first rule and the one which matters is that you shall follow instructions. That applies also to SP12. You know the consequences of failure to follow instructions.'

'I will arrange contact,' answered RS349.

Chapter Two

May morning in Cloud Valley. Mist rose from the river and drifted across the alder and willow trees on Heron Island. To the west a train, a thin blue line, streaked along the embankment. On the valley slopes to the East a farm tractor chugged over the fields.

Here on the island all was quiet, still and secret. But behind the wall of green bushes, in a small open space, someone was at work.

In front of a long, low, battered brick shed stood a workbench, littered with tools and equipment. And behind the table stood a figure dressed in sweater and jeans: male, female – it was impossible to say. The expression on the youngish face was pleasant but neutral.

With a swift movement, the sweater was shrugged off over the head. A bare arm reached for one of the tools on the bench. Then with a gesture of impatience the tool was dropped on the bench, the figure raised both arms and lifted the head from its shoulders and placed it on the grass.

Above the shoulders appeared a narrow metal panel, mounted on slender struts. Rainbow colours flowed across it, shifting from green to yellow, then back to green and then blue. One arm was raised to the bare torso. A light pressure from the fingers and the surface of the chest swung open to reveal a grey metal surface.

As the spectrum panel switched to indigo, the hand

11

picked up the tool again and began to work on the grey surface.

When the figure was at last satisfied, the tool was laid down, the torso cavity closed, the head replaced, then the chest covered again by the sweater.

SP12, self-programming robot from planet Zarnia, was ready for another day.

Turning from the table, SP12 moved smoothly and swiftly towards a lean, grey capsule lying in the grass in the shadow of the shed. As the robot approached, the capsule's top surface opened, a section of the casing swung up and revealed a screen topped by a small revolving disc.

Slowly, carefully, SP12 checked the speed of the disc, noted the presence of the train, the tractor. The dish revolved again. There was no one else within a quarter of a mile.

Few people came to Heron Island. Its small lakes – old gravel pits – and ruined buildings were ignored by anglers. Those who came by chance soon gave up the struggle with the tangle of bramble, bindweed and dense thorn bushes, and went away again.

It was an ideal place for SP12 to make base and carry out the Zarnian Experiment. The robot's position was known only to the four young Earth bios SP12 had selected. And they, the robot knew, would never reveal the secret to anyone else.

That was a remarkable thing. But after two months in Cloud Valley, SP12 knew how remarkable its people were, and had ceased to be surprised.

He knew these young people by their names – Kate, Rachel, Craig and Ash. They, disliking numbers, had nicknamed the robot

Spencer: self-programming-eco-neural-computer-equipped-robot. Not entirely accurate, thought SP12 – nothing on this planet seemed entirely accurate, but ingenious and imaginative.

One thing Spencer had learned in Cloud Valley, sharing the lives of the Four, was to expect the unexpected. That was what made this Experiment interesting. Risky too, risky, but fascinating. Every day brought new experiences, new knowledge – and new dangers.

Spencer gradually extended the range of the bio-sensor until it began to pick up more bios. He identified them swiftly – a family on a boat working their way through an unmanned lock, the water bailiff on his scooter checking the river banks, an old man out for a morning stroll with his dog, anglers bent over rod and line.

All these the robot ignored, and instead looked for the Four to check where they were, one by one. But there was to be no contact. Today Spencer was observing, watching what they were doing when unaware that they were being observed.

The robot knew the two girls and two boys well – but not well enough. Only when the last detail of behaviour and reaction to each situation had been recorded would the experiment be complete. Time was passing. The experiment had a deadline. But haste was unwise. These bios, unlike their Zarnian counterparts, were not predictable by normal logic. Understanding them could not be hurried.

Just as the sensor homed in on the first of the Four, Spencer stopped still. A new sound had registered, a distant clatter and thud in the air – coming nearer.

After a split second's hesitation, the robot closed down the capsule and moved into the shelter of the bushes. In that instant the grey of the capsule began to alter to varying shades of green. The equipment on the old workbench altered colour too, to match its scarred brownness.

Now the thudding sound grew louder. Over the island, blades whirling, came a low-flying police helicopter.

The crew, on their way to monitor rush hour traffic on the bypass, whose giant concrete legs strode across the valley to the south, looked out idly from the cockpit. They saw below them the twin branches of the river gleaming faintly through the rising mist, the flash of sunlight on the gravel pits, the dense green undergrowth, the deserted lock, the ruined lock-keeper's cottage. They never noticed the light green gap of the clearing, with its old brick shed – and its secret.

Five seconds later, the helicopter was away to the south. The capsule slowly emerged from its camouflage and the robot moved back to study the screen once more.

First, thought Spencer, I will study Ash. Once more the dish revolved and the screen began to traverse the valley moving north and west towards the railway embankment, the scrubland, the old glasshouses, littered dump and scrap yard and the back streets of the riverside town of Clayford.

Near the arches of the bridge rose a small block of flats, old and grey. Spencer raised the level of the vision until it focussed on the top storey. And there it rested.

Chapter Three

Ash leaned on the balcony wall and looked along the valley. This was his best time: the whole day before him and his world – Cloud Valley – spread out below. Mist blurred the view but he knew the sun would soon break through. It was going to be fine.

Below he saw the arches. Beneath the arches lay Bozzie's scrap yard, an Aladdin's cave of scrap from every sort of machine. That would be his first port of call, to look over the new load delivered yesterday. In return for first pickings, Ash would help with repair work. The scrap dealer knew Ash had a way with engines.

As he raised the old binoculars hanging round his neck someone tugged at his jacket. He looked down and gave a snort of mock disgust.

'Go away – pest.'

His little sister, still in pyjamas, tugged at his jacket again, raised her large dark eyes to his and answered firmly:

'Don't be rude. I'll tell Mama.'

Ash shivered. 'Oh, please don't. She will beat me.'

His sister squealed with laughter. From the kitchen his mother called, 'Ash, don't say such things.'

'Oh yes,' crowed the girl. 'Let me see through your glasses or Mama will beat you – very hard.'

Ash sighed loudly and lifted her onto a stool so

that her head just reached over the top of the wall. Now he held the binoculars to her eyes.

'Ooh, I can see something. Over the river. A big house.'

'Has it got a red roof?'

'Yes, it has.'

'That's where Kate lives. You've seen her. She is tall and fair . . .'

'I know. She is the bossy one . . .'

'Sh,' called their mother.

Ash laughed. 'Right. She does not care what anyone thinks. She tells them what to do –'

'Do they do it?'

'Sometimes.'

'What is she doing now?'

'In bed, I expect. Why don't you go back to bed, like Kate?'

From down the valley came a faint popping sound.

'Can you hear that?' he asked.

'Like a gun?'

'No, that's a bike.'

'Oh, I know!' His sister grew excited. 'That is Craig. I like Craig. He tells stories. When is he coming again?'

'When you behave yourself. That means never.'

'Ash,' called his mother. 'Don't tease.'

'Oh, she knows I don't mean it – much.'

'You have lots of friends,' went on his sister, 'Kate, and Craig, and Rachel. Where did you find them?'

'Oh, here and there,' he answered. He knew this was not quite the truth. He was hiding the truth. How he met his three friends was a secret he had

16

to keep as long as Spencer, who had brought them together, remained in the valley.

Ash gently took the glasses from his sister, lifted her carefully down from the stool and turned to go. His mother called, 'Are you going out?'

'Just down to the yard.'

'Be careful, there are dangerous people down there.'

He laughed. 'Don't worry. Rodder and his friends are being – taken care of. He's still in hospital, and the other thugs – the police have got them.'

'All the same, Ash. They nearly burned this place down.'

'Nearly, nearly. They were caught, weren't they?'

'Yes,' sighed his mother, 'just in time. We never found out who phoned the police, did we?'

'No.' Ash grinned to himself. He knew who'd alerted the police that desperate night when he and his friends had run up the valley to try and stop Rodder's gang from torching the flats. But that was part of the secret.

His sister held him back.

'You never showed me where Rachel is. Is she still in bed at school like Kate?'

He laughed. 'Not Rachel. She'll be up early, at the big locks with her Grandad. Or maybe on the river.'

Chapter Four

The little boat swung on its mooring rope, the river current tugging gently at it. A girl sat, hands resting on the oars.

She was squarely built; her cheeks, half covered by the long hair, were red, and the eyes dark brown, keen, but sad.

Just now the eyes were gazing downstream towards a clump of reeds. In the shallows stood a long-legged grey bird, fierce eyes on the water. Rachel had spotted the heron just as she was about to push out the boat. Now she waited, still as the heron itself, to see it strike at the fish swimming just below the surface. The thought of the cruel beak stabbing down made her shudder inside, but still she watched. All the life of the valley fascinated her. She took it all in; there was little she missed or did not know.

This morning she had tried to get Kate to join her for a row on the river. But Kate stayed in, pretending she was working on the programme for the Family Week concert. More likely she was still in bed. For someone bursting with energy Kate could be incredibly lazy.

Incredibly laid-back, too. All the girls in the school had begun to be wound up as Family Week came nearer and the place would swarm with parents. Most would pretend to be indifferent to Family Week. But Rachel knew that underneath there was anxiety. Would both parents turn up, would either of them? Would they be talking when they did turn up?

For Kate it was simple. Her parents wouldn't be there. They were deep in the African rain forest engaged in one of the scientific safaris that made them world famous. And Kate was happy with that. The further away, the better, she said flippantly.

For Rachel it was simple, too. Her parents would not be there. But she would not feel like Kate. Her parents had gone – deep into a dark place in her memory, on the other side of a door she kept closed.

To open it again was to see flames and smoke, the blaze and the agony as the car spun and rolled and she was thrown clear and they were not.

Without thinking, her hand went up to brush back her hair, revealing a network of scars across the left side of her face, vanishing into the neck of her shirt, then showing again, red, white on her lower arm.

This did not happen often now. Months of peace at Highwood School, the friendship of Kate – and of Ash and Craig – had given her the confidence to forget her injuries. Yet they were there still and at the end of the summer she would be going back into hospital for more operations.

They would work wonders on her face: like new, said Gran. The thought filled her with sudden dread. What was new like? How would she look to others? Would they still stare, or (which was worse) throw a quick glance, then pretend they weren't looking?

In the last weeks the peace of mind her new friends had brought her had begun to slip away. She had begun to dream the old dreams at night, of flight and red flames clutching out of the dark, while she struggled to wake and escape. Then she would lie in the dark with tears slipping down.

One night in her nightmare she had run and run. And woke to find herself not in bed but standing in the doorway, while Kate sleepily asked: 'Is that you, Ray?'

She'd made some excuse about going to the loo. But she knew she'd walked in her sleep. How far had she gone? Had she been roaming round the school?

She did not tell anyone, especially not the sympathetic staff at Highwood. She had come to the school by chance – a 'chance' organised by Spencer hacking into clinic computers. Ms Hardy, Head of Highwood, had agreed she could stay. It would be a challenge for the school.

Suppose they felt it was too much of a challenge, that her problem needed treatment they could not give? The thought made her cold inside.

She must hang on, cling on to what she had, at least till summer ended. She felt that if they sent her away from Highwood now that would be the end.

The heron's beak swept from side to side. Then, as her eyes turned to the bird again, it rose and flapped away across the water. She heard the helicopter's clatter and made a wry face. The valley was a quiet place, but always being invaded by the world.

The machine passed over heading towards the bypass. Then the valley was still again, except for the long whistle of the train along the distant hump of the embankment. Train sounds seemed part of the valley, the helicopter noise seemed alien, unwanted.

In the silence she heard the faint pop of a machine beyond the scrubland across the water. She frowned. Bikers were out, tearing down the hollows, ploughing through the streams, kicking up the paths. They'd no right to spoil the place.

Then she stopped, smiled wryly. She had a shrewd notion who the biker was.

Raising her left arm, ignoring the burn scars, she looked at the bracelet on her wrist. It was plain, transparent, like glass or plastic. No one would give it a second glance.

Now she concentrated her thoughts on the links and slowly they clouded over. A second later they cleared and in the clear square showed a face – young, pale, fringed with red hair escaping from a battered helmet. The blue eyes looked challengingly into hers.

'Hello Craig,' she murmured.

Craig straddled his bike and looked down into the hollow. All around thorn bushes cut off the view. He was alone here and liked it that way.

Other bikers used the hollow, but only he got up at the crack of dawn to come here and train. He'd fitted up most of the gear – a plank over the stream, two oil drums with an improvised ramp made from an old door. It was rough and ready but served its purpose.

He was used to rough and ready. He and his Mum lived in a basement just by the embankment. His Dad was making the high life somewhere else. Dad had trained him to ride – to follow him as a champion biker. That was an old dream. Now he was on his own.

No – not quite true. All of a sudden he had friends out of the blue, plus Spencer the Tin Man who'd located this bike on Bozzie's scrap heap, all battered and twisted. And with the help of Spencer and Ash, he'd fixed it.

The sun came through the mist and picked out the silver trim. It was a great little bike.

But training – there he was on his own. No proud father showing him the ropes. And none of his friends could help him. This he had to do himself.

He raised his knee to kick start, then felt a sudden tingle in his wrist. He raised his arm, the jacket sleeve slid back. The bracelet clouded then cleared. Someone spoke in his mind.

'Craig.'

'Rachel.'

He looked at the girl's face in the bracelet link and swallowed his irritation at being interrupted.

'You're up early.'

'Right, this way I get the place to myself.'

She made a face.

'You shouldn't really be running the bike in the hollow, Craig.'

'No?'

'No. The bikers spoil all the paths – and the noise! You ought to train on the circuit.'

'Do me a favour, Rachel. This valley isn't just for twitchers and fishers. Anyway, to train on the motocross you have to be in the club. To get in the club needs money and gear, two things I haven't got. So until I get rich or win the championship – or both, I'm training down here.'

She made another face.

'Sorry, didn't mean to preach.'

'Forget it. Where are you? On the river?'

'Where else?'

'Thought you might be. Where's Lady Kate? In bed?'

'Don't let her hear you calling her Lady Kate. She'll strangle you!'

'I believe you. Look, Rachel. I'm just off over the stream, so, go and wake Kate up and pester her. See you.'

'See you.'

Chapter Five

'Something sensational for Family Week.'

The Head's words ran through Kate's head as she sat in her room. Her teeth pressed into her lower lip. Something sensational was to hand – as it happened. All she had to do was sit down and write a letter.

On the table in front of her lay a magazine – a specialist journal for people working in the wildlife field around the world. It came through the post each month.

A small item stood out.

This year's Wildlife Convention in England promises to be more controversial than usual. New evidence about primate family structures, challenging existing ideas, is likely to be put before delegates.

So important is this evidence that researchers Piers and Helen Falkon have decided not to send papers but to break off from their work in the Zarambete Rain Forest to attend the Convention in person – a rare event for them.

They arrive in England at the end of May, two days before the convention opens.

Kate read the last sentence aloud to herself, then added,

'It is rumoured that they may look in on their stroppy little daughter Kate at Highwood School for hopeless cases where they dumped her to be straightened out before leaving on their latest much publicised forest jaunt.'

Into her mind came a vivid picture – the airport lounge in Nairobi. Her father calm but saying nothing. Her mother anxious and pale beneath her tan, saying:

'Kate, dear. You know you are too old to trail around with us now. You need a proper secondary education. You can only get that . . .' she paused, 'at home.'

'Home?' Kate's voice rose so that other travellers turned and eyed them. Most people there knew Piers and Helen. (Who didn't?) This little family scene was something else.

'Home? We haven't been in England since I was in nursery. It's not home. Here's home. My friends are here.'

'Your African friends are. You'll make new friends over there.'

'Nice white ones, eh?' Kate's voice was shrill. Now her father's smile vanished.

'Stop showing off, Kate. You know that's not the case. You need the sort of education you can't get in Zarambete. You need to go to university, *if* you want to be a scientist as you say.'

Her father stressed the 'if'. Kate knew what he meant. 'Being a scientist' was just more showing off. They glared at one another. Her mother made shushing noises. But by now everyone in the lounge was listening and enjoying it.

'University?' screeched Kate. 'When did you go to university? You learnt everything you needed out there.' She pointed dramatically westwards. 'I can do the same.'

'That's not it, Kate,' her mother murmured.

'No, of course it's not. You just want to bloody well get rid of me – 'cause little Kate's grown up into a great big nuisance, hasn't she?'

She'd made her protest and landed up in Highwood. All that seemed years ago. When she thought of that scene, she was half proud of herself for having spoken her mind, half embarrassed at the sheer childishness of it.

Now her parents were coming over here. They hadn't written to tell her – the scientific journal found out first. They had their priorities. In the back of her mind she guessed they might be afraid of her reaction.

And she? What did she think? She didn't know. She'd come to Highwood in a rage – hating her parents, never wanting to see them again, certainly not wanting this nice, expensive school to straighten her out, so that they could carry on their work without her.

Then suddenly things had changed. She'd found her new friends, sad Rachel, clever Ash, touchy Craig, and Spencer the magic-making Tin Thing. She thought of them all with sudden warmth. She'd found a home and a sort of family here.

She knew what would happen when her parents arrived in England. There'd be a phone call to the school, a discreet ride in a hired car to a luxury hotel and an embarrassed reunion. They'd be relieved to see she was thriving. What a good idea Highwood was, they'd tell themselves. Off

26

they'd go to the Convention and she'd be left flat.

She could cause a sensation. She could invite them back to the school for Family Week, floor all the girls and their Mummies and Daddies or whatever they called themselves.

But she wasn't going to do that. Because that would say: 'OK parents, you're forgiven. I'm proud of you.'

But she wasn't and she couldn't, so she wouldn't.

The door was flung open. Rachel came in grinning.

'Greetings from Craig. He asks are you out of bed yet.'

Kate stared at her. Rachel stopped, stared back.

'What's up, Kate? You look – funny.'

Kate shook herself. Rachel came closer, her face concerned. 'What are you looking at? Has something upset you? Show me.'

'No,' snapped Kate. 'It's nothing.' She slapped the magazine shut, rose from the table, flung it into a drawer and slammed that shut.

'Nothing. *Nothing*,' she repeated while Rachel stared at her, eyes wide.

Chapter Six

Noon on Heron Island. The mist had gone and the sun shone from a cloudless sky, taking the chill from the air.

Spencer sat on an old box in the centre of the clearing, head resting on the grass nearby, artificial legs stretched out. The robot was stripped to the waist, the plastic chest cavity open. At its centre a small light blinked. The solar batteries were recharging. Spencer was sunbathing and the spectrum panel with its green-yellow light indicated watchful reflection. Spencer was at ease.

Inside the metal casing the memory bank analysed the morning's impressions. Craig – neutral. The red-haired boy was training on his bike and thinking of nothing else. Ash – at ease, but thoughtful. Too thoughtful. Ash was thinking about SP12. The robot went over the half-formed questions in the boy's mind.

Why had Spencer landed in Cloud Valley? Why choose such a mixed bag of young people? Why all thirteen-year-olds? What was the Experiment for? Why was planet Zarnia interested in planet Earth? What kind of world was Zarnia? Was it robot-run? What sort of people lived there?

Spencer noted the questions. Some he could answer. One – What was the Experiment for? – he could not.

Rachel – active concern. She was in a state of

tension, her mind disturbed, ranging back to the accident that killed her parents – then forward to the operation to remove her scars. On Zarnia, such surgery would be swiftly carried out, the original features restored, with allowance for minute changes of growth over the time since the accident. But they were on Earth, and this was a matter where no intervention was possible. But Rachel must be watched.

Once before the Experiment had been put at risk when Rachel nearly left the area. Only swift action had averted that – action which went beyond SP12's instructions. But such risks had to be taken to keep the Experiment on course.

Kate – potential crisis. Her situation had suddenly changed and her volatile nature, and active hostility to her parents, raised problems. She had been chosen partly for her dynamic nature, partly because of her detachment from her parents. Now they were about to meet: this spelled trouble.

Trouble yes, but also, great interest. On this planet bios were unpredictable, therefore fascinating.

Spencer rose suddenly, closing the chest cavity and striding to the capsule. A green light winked inside the open casing. The robot stretched out a finger and a panel rose from the centre. The spaceship was calling. That was unusual. The rule was, landing units called.

'SP12 receiving RS349.'

'Negative,' came the response. 'The Initiator is calling.'

'Do not understand.'

'Initiator calling SP12. Is that not clear?'

'Understood. Procedure abnormal. Direct contact between Home Base and Landing Unit against the rule.'

The green lights wavering indicated amusement.

'Correct. As I told RS349, I make the rules and break them as I choose. And so do you, evidently, SP12.'

'Do not understand.'

'You are playing for time – a bio-tactic. To go with your new bio-name, Spencer. You have consistently broken the rules since this Experiment began.'

'I am self-programming.'

'Granted. And eco-neural, part-bio, too. But that does not permit you to change the Experiment.'

'Do not under – '

'Do not try my patience, SP12. You have on your own initiative suspended tests on the bio-contacts. I know your reasons. Never mind them. You will resume testing immediately.'

'Impossible. The bio-contacts will not co-operate. That was made clear in my transmission.'

'Your transmission is received and understood. Your reasoning is excellent. Co-operation must be maintained. And the tests will resume. You will concentrate on the female bio – Kate. An excellent subject, brilliant, independent, erratic, a potentially explosive personality, capable of anything. Splendid material.'

'Not –'

'Do not interrupt me, SP12. You will probe the girl's relationship with her parents – to breaking point. She is ideal for our purpose, but she must be fully detached from her family.'

'Understood. But regret not possible. Renewed tests on one of the Four will result in everyone withdrawing co-operation. An offence against any one is seen as a threat to all.'

'Bizarre behaviour.'

'In bio-terms on this planet, it is called friendship.'

'I know what it is, SP12. It is an obstacle. You will overcome that obstacle.'

'How?'

'Does your memory bank carry information about Guess One, Guess Two, Guess Three?'

'Negative.'

'Perhaps not. This was a game played by young Zarnian bios, when telepathy was – more spontaneously used. Each player seeks to deceive its opponent while guessing what the other's thoughts are or will be.'

'This was before the Trans-time on Zarnia.'

'Correct, before things changed. The game, with its psycho-risks, is now illegal. But it may be played on other planets where Zarnian law does not apply. Put the girl Kate to the test and make sure she does not know it – and neither do the others.'

'This will put the group and the Experiment at risk.'

'Not if you are successful in the game play.'

'It is an unacceptable risk.'

'I decide what is acceptable. You will carry out the instruction.'

'And if I fail?'

'Remember my other name. I am Initiator and Terminator. I have your de-activation code. I can destroy you, and *that*' – the screen rippled – 'will mean something to an eco-neural robot. You have feelings, of a sort.'

'De-activation will abort the Experiment.'

'De-activation will follow the Experiment – at my discretion and depending on your response.'

'I am equipped to take my own decisions.'

'Then decide to follow instructions and prolong your useful existence.

'Now, the girl Kate, take careful note . . .'

Chapter Seven

Kate woke in the early dawn. She had slept badly. Her mind had been at work, going round and round the problem since she had read the item in the magazine now hidden in the drawer. What to do? What to do?

Her eyes opened. Faint light showed through the curtain. Then she raised herself vigorously from the bed. Silhouetted against the grey of daybreak was a dark figure.

Kate shot out of bed.

'What are you . . . ?' she began. Then she collapsed back on to the bed, half angry, half laughing.

'Rachel, you idiot. You scared the socks off me. What are you up to?'

Her room-mate drew the cutain aside and turned. Now the light was on her face, Kate saw how pale she was. The eyes were dark patches in the white. She rose and moved swiftly across the room to put her arm around her friend.

'What's wrong? Couldn't you sleep?'

Rachel put her head against Kate's shoulder, then pulled away again. She whispered, 'Bad dreams, that's all.'

Kate looked at her shrewdly. 'Dreams? Come on, Rachel. It's more than that. Is it the . . .' She hesitated. 'The ops?'

Rachel shook her head vigorously. 'Not really – honestly. I don't . . . think of them.' She bent her head again, then burst out, 'I think I'm going funny.'

'Rachel!' Kate's voice rose. 'Don't be so bloody stupid.' Her hand went to her mouth. 'I'm sorry. But you're *not* going . . . it's just – things, isn't it?'

Rachel faced her. The scars on the left side stood out harshly from the pallor of her cheeks. The eyes were calmer, serious.

'I'm sleepwalking.'

The giggle almost escaped Kate's lips. She straightened her face with an effort.

'Rachel – come on!'

'It's true. I wake up and I'm not in the room. I'm somewhere else, in the passage, on the stair. I think it's a dream and try to go to sleep again. Then I feel the floor cold under my feet. I stretch out my hand, feel the walls. And I know I've got out of bed and wandered about without knowing it.'

'Have you told anyone? Shouldn't you go to Matron? She'll give you something.'

'Oh, no. I don't want anything. It'd bad enough without taking things. No, *no*.' Rachel's eyes sparked. Kate was taken aback.

'But Rachel, if you talked to someone, it might help.' She put a hand on Rachel's arm. The muscles stiffened.

'It helps talking to you. But if I talk to – them – you know what'd happen.' Rachel's voice was quieter. 'They'd send me away. I'm only here – on sufferance . . .'

'Rachel. That's not true. Hardy and the others want you here.'

'I know they do. Good for the school. But I'm an

experiment. If things get difficult, they won't be able to cope. They'll send me somewhere . . .' The voice was a whisper now, '. . . where they deal with cases like mine . . .'

Kate pulled Rachel away from the window. 'Come on, Ray. Get dressed. Let's go down to the river, for a row. Then get breakfast. You'll feel better. Anything but this kind of silly talk – come on.'

As they entered the dining room the tables were full. Everyone was talking at once. This was unusual. Breakfast was a time for silence, surly grunts, one-word remarks. But today there was an air of excitement.

Kate raised an eyebrow. At the centre of the most talkative group she saw the pink face and blue, darting eyes of Adrienne. Kate caught Rachel's arm and held her back. Adrienne had not seen them yet and Kate wanted to know what was going on.

'I tell you I saw it.'

'Where?' gasped several voices.

'It came out of the common room and sort of glided along towards the Head's office. Then it just vanished.'

'What were you doing there?' demanded óne girl.

'Oh, poor Addy,' put in another, 'weak bladder.' There was a shriek of laughter. Adrienne's cheeks grew pinker.

'Shut up, you lot,' said the first girl. 'This is serious stuff. I mean this is all Highwood needs to rate as a school – a ghost.'

'Oh, there *is* a ghost.' An older, bespectacled

girl was speaking. 'It's been seen before – but by the river.'

'Oh, tell.'

'It was years ago. I mean before Hardy and Barker and the "be nice" regime. This place was like Colditz. A girl fell for a teacher, started sending letters and presents.'

'Ha,' came a snort, 'catch anybody in their right mind having a crush on the staff.'

When the laughter died, the girl went on: 'The boss found out. The teacher got the elbow – though it wasn't her to blame –'

'And the girl. What happened to her?'

'They were going to send her home but she threw herself in the river.' The voice sank dramatically. 'So every now and then she's seen roaming around near the water.'

'Ooh. Now she's come indoors.'

Adrienne tried to regain the centre of attention. She raised her voice. 'The funny thing is, this figure looked so familiar somehow. It walked sort of shoulders bent, head on one side, like . . .'

'Like what?'

'Well, like Rachel, to be honest. I mean –'

As if on cue, Adrienne turned and raised a hand to her mouth. 'Oh, no. I'm terribly sorry, Rachel. That was tactless. I didn't see you. I didn't mean –'

Kate pushed her way to the table. 'Course you did, you little slug. Now change the subject and pass the toast. Come on, Ray. I'm starving.'

But Rachel had turned and run from the room.

Chapter Eight

For the next few days the Highwood ghost dropped from meal-time conversation. Kate persuaded Rachel to forget the incident at the breakfast table and take her place in the dining room.

At first there would be a lull in the talk as they walked in, but soon the chatter recommenced as if all were normal. Adrienne did not raise the matter again, not out of tact but because she was uncertain what Kate might do.

Instead she bided her time. She had old scores to work off against Kate. She had always come off worse, but she had hopes. So she waited. No other girl felt strongly enough on the matter, so it seemed to drop out of sight.

Kate put her own problem to one side and concentrated on boosting Rachel's spirits, chatting constantly about anything that came into her head, urging her friend to take long walks in the valley, or row on the river. Slowly it seemed Rachel was becoming calmer.

But this was only an interval in the drama, Kate discovered. Talk of ghosts dwindled but now something else more real – and more unpleasant – began to take its place.

Girls started to talk of things missing from their rooms, small items: a pen, an earring, a magazine. Nothing valuable but still disturbing. At first people spoke of things missing, and only as the days passed was the word stealing used. Once started, the subject of conversation caught on.

It surfaced again at breakfast time. And again it was Adrienne who started the hare.

'It must have been at night,' she remarked, suddenly raising her voice to gather the audience. 'I used the pen to write to Daddy just before I went to sleep. When I got up, it was gone.'

She eyed the foot of the table, where Kate and Rachel sat. Kate's eyes took in the tense face of her friend and she struck quickly.

'Come on, Adder. Ghosts don't nick things. You dropped it in your drawers. Just shake around a bit, it'll drop out again.'

The laughter stung Adrienne. She hit back.

'I know things like that don't bother you, Kate. But this was a present from Daddy. I use it to write to him.'

She looked round the table. 'Who would steal something like that?'

'Dry your tears, Addie,' said Kate. 'It'll turn up.'

'You can joke,' said another girl more quietly. 'But things *have* gone missing. Some may have been mislaid, but not all. Someone is nicking, that's what. As you say, ghosts don't, so it must be a someone.'

'Someone from outside,' replied Kate calmly.

'Surely, Kate,' said Adrienne, sweetly reasonable, 'no one would find it worth their while to come in from outside and steal trifles.'

'Addie dear, your pen isn't a trifle,' Kate countered, but she knew she was losing ground. Adrienne pushed her advantage.

'It must be someone in school. Perhaps,' she

38

added slowly, eyes flickering, 'someone who isn't aware what she's doing. You know like the old biddies shoplifting. Someone who's a bit – well, funny.'

'Oh Addie, darling,' Kate drawled. 'We're all a bit funny, aren't we? That's why our dear parents dropped us on Highwood.'

Adrienne's eyes sparked.

'Speak for yourself, Kate. My fa – parents sent me here because the school has a high reputation. It's not a clinic, is it?'

Her eyes wavered slightly as if to take in Rachel who looked down at her half-eaten meal. Kate reached under the table to squeeze Rachel's hand.

'Tell you what, Addie, if it's so important, let's do something practical, instead of making insinuations.'

Adrienne's lip tightened. 'Like what?'

'Like keeping watch. Night patrol.'

'Ms Hardy wouldn't go for that,' put in another girl.

'Who,' asked Kate, 'is going to bother the boss about it, eh? Anyway. I'll take the first shift tonight. Anybody prowling gets clobbered. Tomorrow we all come on identity parade and see who has the claw marks.'

Despite her bravado, Kate was uneasy. But, despite her uneasiness, when she lay down on her bed, fully clothed, that night she fell instantly asleep.

She woke suddenly. The bedside clock told her it was 2 a.m. She cursed herself, looked round and stood up quickly. Rachel's bed was empty, the sheets turned back, the window open and the curtains blowing in the breeze.

Outside the moon was up but shining fitfully through moving cloud.

Without hesitation Kate climbed out, dropped to the ground and moved swiftly across the lawn. At the low wall beyond, she looked back. The school was in darkness. Another second and she was dropping down the slope towards the river, picking her way through the bushes. She reached the water quickly. The river was quiet and still.

Then her ears caught a faint noise behind her. She turned so swiftly she stumbled, saved herself with both hands on the grass, then scrambled forward. A ray of moonshine showed a crouching figure ahead of her.

She almost called out, but stopped in time, then pushed on up the slope. Now there was another faint noise ahead, a light crunch of gravel underfoot. But nothing more.

Ahead of her rose the school building. Two windows were open: the room she had left, and the common room.

She leaned over the common room windowsill in time to hear the inner door closing. Scrambling over the sill she crept across the floor and out into the corridor.

So quickly did she move, her quarry was only a little way ahead, crouching outside the Head's study.

Kate halted, raised her arm and signalled Rachel on her bracelet. The link clouded, tinged with irridescent light, then went blank again. Strange.

Though her head had been bent for a second only, when she lifted it again the figure had gone. Inside the office? Along the passage? Through a window?

Silently she crept up the stairs and back to her room. As she opened the door she heard someone gasp. She switched on the light. Blinking, in pyjamas, Rachel sat on the bed.

'Where have you been?' Both spoke at once.

'I've been round the school looking for you,' whispered Kate. 'What were you up to?'

'I – I . . .' stammered Rachel, 'only went to the loo. When I got back, you'd gone.'

'Yes. On night patrol. Listen, Rachel. Are you sure you only went to the loo? You didn't go down to the river or into the common room?'

'No, no no,' answered Rachel, distressed. 'I'm – sure I didn't.'

She jumped from the bed and grasped Kate's arm. 'You didn't see me . . .' It was half statement, half question.

'I called you on the bracelet. Why didn't you answer? There was no trace, you cut out completely. That could only happen if you were asleep.'

'I don't remember anything, Kate.' Rachel's voice was a whisper. 'Oh Kate, I don't know what I'm doing . . . What's happening to me?'

Chapter Nine

That evening Rachel sat at the table in their room absorbed in colouring her sketch of the heron. Kate had persuaded her to work rather than brood, but it had taken time. She looked at the sad face with its fringe of hair for a moment before tiptoeing out. In the end she knew Rachel would have to fight this battle with her fears and anxieties, alone.

In the passage outside, Kate tucked her copy of *Star Trek – The Next Generation* under her arm and headed for the common room. It would probably be crowded and difficult to concentrate on her reading, but she needed a change of scene.

And that was what she got.

Chairs were drawn into a circle. Adrienne, Kate realised, was holding one of her audiences. She was in full flow, little pink nose in the air, finger upraised as if conducting an orchestra of gasps of amazement and giggles from her audience.

For a second Kate was tempted to interrupt with some gem of caustic wit, but she kept her mouth shut and found a deep armchair in a corner, turned its back to the circle and settled down. Adrienne was so absorbed Kate almost believed she had entered the room unobserved.

She soon realised her mistake.

Adrienne, who had been retailing some piece of scandal about a member of staff, suddenly switched the topic to Family Week.

'Would you believe, Daddy's decided to come after all? He was going to be incredibly busy, finishing this book. But after all it's going like a dream. So he's going to be here for the concert.'

'How super for you Adrienne. He'll be able to see you do your big scene, won't he?'

'I should die,' gasped someone, 'with him in the audience. I mean, he's used to mixing with all the top show business people, isn't he Adrienne?'

'Not *all*,' Adrienne's voice was reproachful. 'There are some he wouldn't be seen dead with.'

'I expect he knows too much about them. It must be incredible to be in on all their secrets.'

'Do you think your father would agree to give a Celebrity talk, Adrienne, at the end of Family Week?' asked one girl.

'Oh yes,' the whole group urged. 'What a terrific idea.'

'No chance, I'm afraid. He'll be off to the States by then – another project.'

Kate squirmed at the slight drop in Adrienne's voice – not quite a sigh. She shrugged herself deeper into the chair and tried to lose herself in the book. But Adrienne had not finished yet.

Her voice rose once more. 'Besides, I should guess Ms Hardy will be hoping to land someone else for Celebrity Night.'

There was a hush. Kate tensed.

'Who, Adrienne?'

'Piers and Helen Falkon, that's who.'

Some force inside her shot Kate out of the chair to land her behind the circle.

'What's that supposed to mean?'

The suddenness and sharpness of the words shocked the other girls into silence, but Adrienne seemed prepared.

'Oh Kate, I'm sorry. If I'd know you were sitting there I wouldn't have spoken.' She paused for effect. 'I just happened to know, Piers and Helen are going to be around for Family Week.'

'How the hell would you know that?'

Kate knew she was going over the top but could not control her words. Now even Andrienne was nervous.

'I saw it in *World Wildlife*.'

'Since when did you subscribe to *World Wildlife*?' Kate leaned forward. Adrienne had recovered herself. She reached down by the side of the chair and held up a magazine. It was open at the centre page and the news about Kate's parents was ringed in red.

Kate snatched the journal. 'What are you doing with this? I was reading it.'

'But Kate,' Adrienne's voice was smooth. 'I found it lying on the floor, just like that.'

'You –' Kate burst out, then stopped. She spoke more quietly, coldly. 'I should think it unlikely their work at the convention will allow them time to come here, even for the chance of meeting you.'

As she spoke she knew the words were childish and stupid. But the incident had scrambled her brain. A whole train of possibilities had been set rolling, each one more disagreeable than the last.

She left the room in silence. But as she reached the stairs she heard muffled whispers and giggles.

* * *

Rachel, putting the finishing touch to her drawing, looked up wide-eyed as Kate burst in, holding the magazine.

'Do you know how this found its way from my drawer over there into the common room and into that slug Adrienne's hands?'

Rachel's mouth opened in suprise. She stuttered:

'I – I don't know Kate. How can I? I saw you reading it and I saw you stick it in the drawer. I haven't seen it since.'

'Are you sure?' Kate's voice was hard.

Rachel stared. The scars stood out red in her paling face.

'What do you mean, Kate? What do you mean?'

Chapter Ten

The crowd outside Valley School slowly dispersed, climbing into parents' cars, pushing their way towards the High Street, scrumming around the buses in the car park.

Two figures moved away from the ruck and walked slowly down one of the side streets. One, small, square-shouldered, in faded sweater and jeans, pale-faced and red-haired; the other by contrast, tall, dark-skinned, hook-nosed, his worn anorak hanging open. Others barely gave them a glance as they separated from the crowd.

Ash looked sideways at Craig.

'Coming back home for a bit?' he asked hesitantly.

Craig shrugged. 'Yeah, OK. Just for a bit. I want to get off down the Valley with the bike.'

Ash grinned. 'You don't think of anything else, these days. How's it going?'

'Not bad. Be better if I could work on the course up at the club.'

'Why not?'

'You're joking. Having the ready to join would be something. And I can't join the club without the gear. They'd die laughing.'

Ash nodded. Being short of cash was something he understood.

'If you got in the club, you'd beat any of 'em.'

'Even Stevens?'

'Him as well, the bighead.'

'He's good, you know.'

'You're ace, Craig.'

'He's got a better bike.'

'Correction. He's got a newer bike. But I reckon since Spencer fixed yours up, there isn't much in it.'

Craig grinned. 'Not many'd know it came off Bozzie's dump,' he said. 'Tell you what, Ash, will you have a look at the tuning for me?'

'Sure. Will you come back first and tell my sister a story? If I let you go, she'll skin me.'

'Why not? Two thousandth episode of Monster of Cloud Valley.'

Both laughed as they turned the corner. Ahead the road ended by the old tower block where Ash and his family lived. Craig lived nearby in a basement flat with his mother.

'Stevens keeps a low profile, these days,' observed Ash.

'Don't wonder,' answered Craig. 'With Rodder in dock and his big friends in the slammer, he has nobody to mind him, does he?'

Ash nodded. 'He was lucky they didn't shop him after that fire. He'd be in lumber, if anyone talked. That's why he keeps clear of us.'

'Well it can stay that way. Peace and quiet is what I want, and get on with my training. Even Spencer's keeping a low profile these days.'

'Yes,' said Ash, 'ever since he got fixed up with his base on Heron Island, he's keeping very quiet.'

'Have you tried to contact him?' asked Craig.

'Yeah, a couple of times. Things I wanted to ask him,' returned Ash. 'But no answer.'

'Think he's still there?'

'Oh yes, the power's still on – the bracelet's working. But nothing from Spencer.'

'So, he's busy. Does it matter?'

'It's strange, that's all. He must be up to something.'

They reached the foot of the flats, when Ash stopped Craig.

'Listen, have you heard from Rachel?'

'No. Not for some while. We chatted a bit once. She told me off for using my bike in the hollow and destroying the environment. So I told her a thing or two. Nothing special – just typical Rachel.'

'I'm worried about her.'

'Oh, why?'

'She called me earlier today. Seemed very upset. Wants us to meet on the river above the weir pool on Saturday.'

'So?'

'She didn't say much, but I think she needs help. Something's wrong at school. She reckons she's being accused of stealing,' he paused, 'and Kate doesn't seem to want to know.'

Craig shrugged. 'That figures. But,' he went on cautiously, 'Rachel does get wound up easily about things. Probably by the weekend, it'll all be over. I could do without meeting up this time.'

Ash was firm. 'I know what you mean. But we can't let Rachel down. We've got to find out what it's all about.'

He led the way up the steps to the flat.

'Come on, mate. I can smell baking.'

* * *

Later they stood on the balcony looking down over the valley. Ash's sister, still demanding another story, had been put to bed. In the lighted kitchen, Ash's mother stood by the sink. His father had gone off to the restaurant.

Reluctantly Craig turned to go. Ash followed him to the head of the steps.

'Listen. I'll come down to your place early Saturday and have a look at the bike, then we'll go down the river and meet the girls.'

'OK. See you.'

'Hang about,' said Ash in surprise, holding up his arm. 'Someone's coming through.'

Both boys stared at the bracelet on Ash's wrist. The transparent links had clouded but the whiteness had a rainbow tinge.

'Hey, Spencer,' said Craig.

'Uh huh,' answered Ash as the link cleared. 'Look.'

Kate's face, grinning broadly, took shape.

'Hi.'

'Hi,' both boys responded. But not a word was spoken.

'Listen. This Saturday meet. Let's call it off, hey? I know Rachel asked for it, but we're both wanted for this school thing, so . . . See you around. OK?'

Before either boy could answer, the image had faded. The link cleared.

'That's it, then,' said Craig. 'We leave it.'

Ash shook his head: 'No. There's something funny going on. I want to know what.'

'So?'

'So, we go down there on Saturday, anyway.'

Chapter Eleven

Ms Hardy looked at Kate across her office desk and grinned.

'Well, you've done a pretty effective job on the Family Week programme. Bit of everything there – music, drama and, what is most important, everyone, but everyone, is involved in some way. You've been a real diplomat.'

'Yes,' said Kate recklessly, 'even having Adrienne and Sheena doing the balcony scene from *Romeo and Juliet*. Hope there aren't any Shakespeare lovers in the audience.'

She could see Sheena as Romeo. Sheena was dark, slim and not a bad actor. But the thought of Adder as Juliet, that little pink porker pouting over the cardboard balcony, was enough to make one throw up.

The Head coughed. 'That is what a school concert's about – everyone doing their bit. It isn't just talent.'

'Say that again,' murmured Kate, but to herself. Aloud she said: 'We could do with one item to round off the evening, something really good, professional, something that doesn't make you grind your teeth.'

'Have you any ideas, Kate?'

'To be honest, Ms Hardy, no. But there's still a little time left.' She looked at the Head. 'I might think of something. Is that OK?'

She rose to go, but Ms Hardy raised a hand and she sat down again.

The Head spoke slowly. 'Thinking of something special – is there a chance that your parents might join us for Family Week? I'm thinking of the Celebrity Evening at the end of the Week.'

Kate burst out, 'Why can't Adrienne keep her trap shut?' Then she stopped as she saw the look of astonishment on Ms Hardy's face. She sat down again.

'I mean,' she faltered, 'I didn't see how you could know . . .' She fell into silence as the Head spread out on the desk top the inside pages of one of the tabloid newspapers.

'That's how I know, Kate.'

Across the page was a huge photograph – a well-known one, of her mother and father, in safari gear, handing a baby gorilla back to its mother.

The caption was brief, but memorable:

Time out with baby gorilla, for eco-stars Piers and Helen Falkon, due in England shortly to tell the world how families work in the wild. And maybe to see how their daughter, who we hear is tucked away in a very special school for difficult dears, is getting along. Easier with gorillas, isn't it?

Kate gasped, 'How did they know?' Then, 'That slug Adrienne must have phoned them!'

'Kate! What *is* this about Adrienne?'

Kate quickly described the scene in the common room. Ms Hardy shook her head.

'I don't think so, somehow, Kate. You see, I took a chance and phoned the paper. To ask where they got the information. They said – of course – we don't reveal our sources.'

'Perhaps they're guessing about the school,' said Kate.

'I don't think so. They were rather sly. You see I didn't give my name, but they said: "I assure you, madam, it is no-one from your school".'

'They must be saving that bit up till my parents arrive.'

'The point is, Kate, it might help a little if you persuaded your parents to come here publicly. That would make the story a bit ridiculous, wouldn't it?'

Kate stared at the Head. 'I'm not sure if they would want to, and –' she paused a little – 'I'm sure I don't want them to.'

'Oh!'

Kate went on: 'You know I never wanted to come here. They dumped me.'

The Head's eyes narrowed, but Kate kept talking. 'They said I needed a secondary education at home, to prepare for university.'

'Don't you?'

'No,' Kate's tone was contemptuous. 'Look at my class reports. In science subjects I could get into university this year, if I wanted –'

She pressed on before the Head could interrupt. 'What I need to learn I could learn out there. I was free there. I worked. They treated me as an equal.'

Kate looked out of the window as if seeing into the distance. 'I mixed with the village children, everyone, went to the Mission school. I spoke three of their languages. I belonged. I was – like a grown up. I could do anything.'

She stopped for breath.

'Then suddenly they decided I was a kid and a bit wild and needed straightening out. They wanted me out of the way. They didn't want me there. I don't want them here.'

Ms Hardy's face softened. 'I know how you feel about Highwood . . .' She opened a drawer, held up a white envelope.

'You remember, Kate, you forged a letter from me telling your parents to remove you.'

Kate looked down.

'But, I felt you'd come to like your time here. You've been a real friend to Rachel, loyal and caring.'

'And Adrienne?' Kate demanded.

The Head smiled. 'I think even Adrienne has done you good. You can't dominate her.'

Kate laughed aloud, but without humour. 'Adrienne.' She tapped the newspaper.

'They said no one from the school, Kate.'

'Well, that smartass father of hers.'

'Kate!' The Head's tone was sharp.

'I'm sorry. Just assuming like father, like daughter.'

'I am sure Mr Dyott has no connection with the Press. He's a well known biographer.'

'Huh,' Kate shrugged.

'There's another thing needing explanation, Kate. How that magazine got from your room to the common room. Who made the markings? Things have been happening in the school . . .'

'I asked Rachel about the magazine,' said Kate. 'She doesn't know.'

'Doesn't know?'

'She couldn't say she hadn't touched the magazine,' Kate rushed on. 'She's been feeling strange lately, nightmares and sleepwalking. Can't remember where she's been.'

'Kate, please be careful what you are saying and thinking. Rachel is under a lot of strain. If things developed in that direction we might not be able to cope with it at Highwood.'

The Head folded the newspaper.

'We would all be sorry if Rachel had to leave.'

Chapter Twelve

'You did *what*?'

Rachel glared at Kate, who, lying idly on the bed, gazed calmly back.

'I told Craig and Ash we wouldn't be coming.'

'You had no right to do that.'

Rachel lifted her arm and stared angrily at her bracelet. Kate flung back the bedclothes, leapt across the room and seized her arm.

'Don't, Ray. They're probably off down the Valley somewhere, with Craig's bike. I know Ash was going to tune the engine. You can't bring them back just for a Saturday chat.'

Rachel broke away, snapping, 'It is not a chat. I asked them to meet us to discuss something important.'

'Like what?'

'Like who is setting me up as some kind of loony creeping round the school stealing things.'

Kate laughed. 'That's a change for the better. A few days ago you seemed to believe it was you. Now it's a set up. We're making progress.'

'Don't do this, Kate. I know I've been sleep-walking. But I don't believe I've been sneaking into people's rooms stealing.'

'Well, it does sound absurd,' said Kate, calmly.

'Absurd? You as good as accused me of stealing your magazine and giving it to Adrienne.'

'I asked if you'd taken it. You couldn't say yes or no.'

'That's how I felt then. I was desperate. Now I feel angry. There must be some explanation. And I want Craig and Ash – yes, and Spencer – to help me find out who. Because nobody here will help me.'

'Spencer? You'll be lucky. He isn't talking to us any more.'

Kate began to dress. 'Come on. We're going out.'

'Going out? You said . . .'

'Yes, out, but not to meet the boys. Miss Barker's taking a group orienteering down to the Country Park. I put our names down. You'll like it. You're good at these things. You know the Valley like the back of your hand. Come on. Show 'em. Wipe the stupid smiles off their faces. They don't know how good you are. They only see you crawling round the place with a miserable expression.'

Kate dragged on her track suit and gave a skip. 'Come on.'

'Did you say, down to the Country Park?'

Kate turned at the change in Rachel's voice. 'Yes, we start at Martin's Farm, then it's off to the jungle.'

'OK, Kate. Look, you go down and tell Miss Barker I'm coming. I'll be with you in a couple of minutes.'

'You won't hide under the bed?'

Rachel snatched up a pillow and hurled it at Kate. But before it had landed the door had closed behind her.

Rachel smiled, listened for a few seconds, then raised her arm.

Miss Barker looked round at the circle of girls in the farmyard.

56

'Listen carefully and look at your maps. See the three red dots? Right? Those are control points. The first is 300 metres north-west of here. The next one is 400 metres north of that. The third is home, that is where Miss Morrell will check you in at the school yard.

'At each control point you'll find a peg board with flags stuck in. Take one. Stick it in your jumper. Don't take more than one each or I'll have your guts for garters. Show your two flags to Miss Morrell, when you get there.

'Now, if you find compass reading difficult and I know some of you can't even find your way to the loo at night, listen carefully again. North-west you can see the Tower blocks near River Road, beyond the railway embankment. North you can see the drag line excavators in the gravel workings. When you reach the second control point you will see the red roof of home.

'Wait for it. Wait for it! I shall be keeping a look out for strays from Witches' Hill.'

'That's about right,' muttered Kate.

'I heard that, Falkon, and shall not forget it. Watch out you don't find yourself hopping around with green and yellow spots all over you. Now, off you go.'

To Kate's surprise, Rachel went off like a rocket, leaving the others staring at their maps.

'Rachel, not so fast,' called Miss Barker. But Rachel was already dodging into the undergrowth.

Baffled, Kate wasted no more time but broke into a run and was soon twisting and turning through the maze of thorn and elder bushes, now bursting with white and pink blossom.

Rachel had vanished. Kate paused and listened for sounds of movement ahead. But all was quiet except for an idiot blackbird warning all comers off his territory.

Kate shrugged and looked at her map. Three hundred metres north-west, in line with the tower blocks. Where were they? Thorn bushes twenty feet high blocked her view. She took out her compass. She'd found her way in thicker scrub than this before.

She pressed on, five, ten, fifteen minutes. The sun was well up and it was warm. Kate felt sweat break out on her neck. The track suit became hot and she pulled the zip down. A branch whipped across her chest and she pulled the zip up again.

She checked the compass. She was off course, swinging south. Through a gap in the bushes she saw in the distance the gaunt crosses and cables of the transformers. That was well south-west, she knew. She about faced and headed north. She must go a good hundred metres to get back in line.

Suddenly she felt a flush of irritation with Rachel for dashing ahead. Then she grinned. Getting her own back, no doubt. Rachel was deep. But this was a touch nasty. That wasn't like Rachel who didn't have a nasty bone in her body. Still, anyone could change, under stress.

Something tugged at her sleeve – branch, bramble. She jerked free without looking. There it was again, grabbing her arm, tugging.

Rachel, grinning slyly, was at her side. With a jerk

of her head she indicated a path to the side almost invisible among the willow and alders.

'Short cut. Come on. This way Barker won't see us. Save time.'

Rachel cheating? But Kate followed. The path twisted and turned; the grass underfoot grew longer, wetter.

They leapt small puddles and a brook. Then they were out in the open. In front was a line of alder trees, tall and graceful, an old grey stone ruined mill and, beyond, the glint of marshes.

'Over here.'

Kate followed. There was a bridge ahead, broken. They leapt the gap and plunged into thick greenery, fern-like plants, reeds four feet high, rushes stiff and tall with fluffy heads, yellow flag irises.

'Where are you taking me?'

'Come on.'

They were in a clearing. Kate stopped. Great jagged columns of stone, broken crumbling walls stood round.

'What's this?'

'Tell you another time. Come on.'

Kate followed, face flushed and red, track suit soaked. She looked at the sun. They were heading west. Some short cut! Open ground again. And now they were on the river bank. Below was a lock. Rachel scrambled down and padded across the swaying footbridge. By the time Kate caught up they were on the tow path, heading north.

'Nearly there,' Rachel called over her shoulder.

Ahead Kate heard a dull roar, then saw the dark timbers and foaming water of the weir. The truth began to dawn on her. Now Rachel was bounding across the catwalk. Kate could only follow, indignant and amused at once.

Across the river, Rachel turned, dodged round a willow clump and dropped down to a small sandy inlet.

Stretched out on the turf were Ash and Craig. Craig looked up.

'Late as usual, Lady Kate.'

'I'll strangle you,' shouted Kate. But she meant Rachel.

Chapter Thirteen

Kate and Rachel flopped on the grass beside the boys, slowly recovering their breath. Kate tugged off her track suit top and mopped her face, then eyed Rachel.

'Sneaky Ray – fooled me all the way.'

Rachel did not return the smile. She answered seriously, 'Well, you cheated.'

'I did?'

'Yes, you did – cancelling the meeting. You never asked me.'

Kate shugged. 'What if I did? Who needs all this drama?'

Rachel looked as if she would explode. Ash looked quickly from one girl to the other, then intervened.

'Look, Kate, what's going on at your school sounds like real trouble for Rachel. It does look as though she's being set up. Someone's trying to get rid of her.'

'Like who?'

Ash was calm. 'Well, like Adrienne. She'd do anything to harm Rachel or you – if she could.'

'Could's the word,' retorted Kate. 'I for one don't believe Adrienne came into our room, rummaged around till she found a mag she never reads with a news item she didn't know about . . . then –'

'Hang about,' interrupted Craig. He had been lying on his back, staring up at the trees. Now he sat up, frowning. 'Are you saying it isn't a set-up?'

Kate was silent. Ash put in: 'Kate, what does it mean?'

Kate looked at the boys, then at Rachel. 'That's the hard bit,' she said slowly, 'That's why I was – trying to get out of this meet.'

'Go on,' Rachel said, between closed teeth.

'OK.' Kate breathed in, then went on, 'Rachel has been sleepwalking. She's upset. So would anybody be. When she's . . . in that state, she could have taken out that magazine, wandered about, left it in the common room.'

'How would I know what was in the mag?' demanded Rachel.

'Perhaps you didn't. But you saw me close it pretty quickly when you came into the room and hide it. That might be enough to . . . sort of trigger –'

'Thanks very much!'

Ash put his hand on Rachel's arm. 'And you think the other thefts might have been done by Rachel – by accident? That's pretty dire.'

Kate sat up. 'These things are possible. The bad thing is, Rachel's upset. A big drama, a big Sherlock Holmes thing will just wind her up more. What she needs is to try and forget it and think about other things – like how good it'll be after the ops – and try and sleep at night. The more fuss we make, the worse it is for her.'

Rachel, face pale, said nothing. Craig rolled over and looked at her.

'That's something. Suppose there was an investigation? Suppose it *was* you? You know what'd happen?'

Rachel bit her lip, nodded.

'Hold on,' said Ash, 'So Rachel accidentally put that mag in the common room. But you're not saying she rang the *Morning Sketch* and gave them that story about your parents?'

Kate laughed. 'No. Don't be silly. But it didn't have to be anybody from the school. The Head says they deny all contact with the school.'

'So you don't think Adrienne did that?'

'Don't know and not really bothered.' Kate stretched out. 'Hey, it's getting really hot.'

'Kate,' Rachel's voice was sharp. 'I won't fall out with you over what you think about those thefts and me. But don't you care if this gutter rag makes trouble for your parents?'

Kate yawned.

'My parents are old enough to look after themselves. That's what they decided about me. They decided it would do me good to cope without them. The same applies to them.'

Craig nodded. 'She's got a point. Big name people have to take a lot of stick.'

'Maybe,' answered Ash, 'but this news item looks bad about Kate as well, and the other people at the school, including Rachel.'

Kate threw off her trainers and, stepping forward, dipped her toe in the water. She shuddered and grinned. 'Hey, it's cold, but not lethal. I'm going in.'

'You're crazy,' said both boys.

'Uh huh,' she answered and stepped aside behind a bush. Her head was still visible over the leaves as she went on talking.

'Look, you three. In four weeks' time, Family

Week will be over and forgotten. So will the fuss. My parents'll come and go – as usual. I shall be here. You lot'll be here. Spencer as well. We'll have fun.'

'And Rachel?'

'Oh, if you like, I'll barricade the bedroom door and make sure she stays in bed – anything but this drama.'

Rachel sprang up. Now her face was fire red. The boys were open-mouthed at the sudden burst of anger.

'I can take it when you rubbish what's happening to me. I know you can be hard as nails. That's the way you get by. I can't be like that. And I can't stand it when you don't care what happens to your parents. If you'd lost them for good you'd see things differently.'

Kate's eyes were blank.

'I *have* lost them. Or rather, they've lost me. Now, I'm having my dip.' She grinned at the boys. 'Last one in's a wimp.'

'You really don't care, Kate. You are so hateful.'

Rachel glared furiously at the boys, who turned away in embarrassment.

'OK,' shouted Rachel, 'if that's how it is!' Tucking in her head to hide her face, she turned and ran along the bank, ducking under the willow branches

'Rachel!' called Ash, jumping to his feet.

'Oh, leave her,' called Kate. Darting suddenly from behind her bush, with a flash of long legs she dived low into the water, surfaced, threw back her hair and mocked the boys.

'What a pair of ci-ssies!'

Craig laughed, got up and peeled off his shirt.

Chapter Fourteen

Miss Barker sat on Witches' Hill, her back to a tree, thermos in one hand, cup in the other, at peace with the world. The valley was spread out before her with its intriguing jumble of wild undergrowth, reed-fringed lakes, scrubland and all the litter of industry: power station, gravel workings, the derelict glasshouses. A fantastic place, she thought.

Why the Highwood girls disliked it, she couldn't think. It took all her powers of persuasion to get them out from the school. They seemed afraid of nature, she thought – except Rachel and Kate. They seemed to revel in Cloud Valley – and disappear into it on every possible occasion. Though what they were up to she could not imagine.

She picked up her binoculars and swung them slowly to and fro across the orienteering course. This side of the river seemed empty – even the stragglers must have reached the school.

A flash of movement down near the weir caught her attention for a moment. Some kids playing in the river. She put down the thermos and picked up the walkie-talkie. The button glowed and she heard Miss Morrell's voice.

''Lo, Jean,' she called.

Miss Morrell, standing on the gravel path behind the school, winced and held the earpiece away from her head.

'This is the electronic age, Kath. You don't have to shout down these things.'

'Sorry. Everybody home?'

'Yes. Bar a couple.'

'Stragglers? Let me guess.'

'You won't. Kate and Rachel.'

'They should have been home hours ago. Rachel can do the route blindfold.'

'Well, she must have done. She's just coming up the slope now, looking hot and bothered.' Miss Morrell broke off a second, then, 'Says she's lost Kate.'

'Lost Kate?'

Miss Morrell moved the earpiece again. 'Lost and lost. Says she left her by the river, above the weir. Between you and me, I think they had a spat. Rachel looked grim.'

Miss Barker grunted, 'OK, leave it with me. I'll track Kate down.'

Miss Barker laid down the walkie-talkie and picked up the binoculars. Now she wasted no time but focussed on the water above the weir, beyond the green mound of Heron Island. As she turned the knob, the swimming figures suddenly became larger, clearer. They swam vigorously, leaping about and splashing each other. She could almost imagine she could hear what they were saying and felt a twinge of envy. Years since she'd gone skinny dipping.

'Oh ho,' she said and stood up. One figure had blondish hair. That's my girl, she thought. But who were the others, one light one dark? Whatever – they were both boys, she was sure. Then she laughed at herself. How could she be sure at this distance?

Swiftly she packed walkie-talkie, thermos and clipboard into her rucksack, swung it on to her shoulder and came down off Witches Hill at a purposeful five miles an hour.

Rachel, on her way to the changing rooms, stopped by the corner of the school buildings. She could hear Miss Morrell on the walkie-talkie. Her fury with Kate had seeped away by now, leaving only a resentful tiredness. She felt guilty – and justified. Kate had no right to be so flippant, so cynical, so hard. Rachel almost did not believe her. Why pretend to be so callous, though? You had to be thick-skinned to even fake it.

Yet Rachel wished she hadn't stormed away from the others. She'd lost the chance to convince the boys and get their help. Kate seemed to twist people round her finger. Was it because she didn't care, or because she knew what she wanted and how to get it? If only I could be like that, she thought.

Miss Morrell was talking about them. She heard the words, 'Left Kate by the river.'

Her guilt returned. If she hadn't been furious she'd not have told Miss Morrell where Kate was. But that wasn't an accident, she'd done it on purpose. She'd behaved like someone in junior school – 'Mi-iss, Kate Falkon's playing in the river with the boys.'

Angry with herself she walked to the changing room. Serve Kate right. Didn't anything bother her? Well, let her get out of this one.

The sound of the words in her head, their childishness stopped her in her tracks. She looked round.

No one was near. She raised her arm and looked at the bracelet. Ah well, better late than never.

'Kate,' she thought.

The bracelet clouded over. Strangely, the white mist was tinged with green and orange. Then it cleared.

'Kate!' She spoke aloud in her exasperation. But the bracelet clouded and cleared again. Had Kate taken the bracelet from her wrist? That couldn't be. Either she wasn't listening or something had gone wrong.

She tried again.

'*Ash.*'

The brown face, eyes blinking, forehead beaded with water, appeared.

'Rachel. You OK?'

'Yes. But you're not. I tried to get Kate.'

'She's here.'

'Well, she's not answering. Listen. One of the Highwood teachers is coming down to look for Kate. You two had better vanish.'

'Aargh.'

Miss Barker pounded over the weir catwalk. She could hear the shouts of the bathers beyond the willows at the river bend. Now she was sure there were boys there.

She came off the catwalk at a run, feeling embarrassed. Still – do the job properly. She slackened pace and walked more lightly. How absurd to creep up on people. However.

She reached the willow clump. Now she could recognise the girl's voice. It was Kate Falkon all right.

But as she reached the bend with its shelving shore she stopped, baffled. There was only one swimmer in the water. It was Kate, mouth open, hands clasped in front of her, her face twisted in a silly grin.

'Kate, what are you up to?'

'Oh hell . . . er, Miss Barker. I was running along the bank and fell in.'

Miss Barker made herself sound stern.

'Did you? Lucky you managed to undress before you hit the water. Come on girl. Get out, get dressed and get back to school. We shall have words.'

Chapter Fifteen

Crouched among the reeds Craig and Ash watched Kate led off up the slope towards Highwood. For a few seconds they each avoided the other's eye then, shaking with laughter, they staggered on to the grass to retrieve their clothes.

Then Ash was serious. 'How did she know Kate was down here with us?'

Craig shrugged. 'How do you think? She must be their minder, making sure they don't mix with the rubbish from Valley school. Did you see the binoculars and walkie-talkie? Morality Patrol.'

'Get off,' Ash grinned. 'They were supposed to be orienteering. She came to find if Kate had gone off course.'

'Well she had, hadn't she? She'll be for the high jump.'

Ash pulled on his jacket. 'Oh, I expect Kate'll talk her way out of this.'

'Sure. She takes it all dead calm, doesn't she?'

'That's what worries me, Craig.' The two were dressed now and walking over the weir bridge. 'Something's wrong and I can't put my finger on it.'

'How d'you mean?'

'This business of Rachel nicking things in her sleep. I don't believe it. Do you?'

'Dunno. Stranger things happen.'

'You're a real friend. I don't believe you do in your sleep what you wouldn't awake. Rachel's not like that.'

'She's all wound up, don't forget.'

'I know. That's why she needs help. That's why I don't get what Kate's up to – pretending not to care about anything.'

'Pretending? How d'you know, Ash?'

Ash looked uncomfortable. 'I just don't see Kate being as rotten as that. It's as though she's playing some game.'

'With us?'

'Maybe. Why, I can't say.'

They stood on the far bank. Craig shifted to and fro. Ash could see he was keen to get back to his bike. He put a hand on Craig's arm.

'I think Spencer's up to something, too.'

'Like what?'

'I don't know. What I do know is that the contact system is very erratic.'

'The bracelets?'

'Right. When you try to get someone, Kate for example, you get this rainbow edge on the link, as though Spencer's coming through, then it clears. But you can't get Spencer anyhow.'

'So?'

'What should he be up to? We told him no more tests, didn't we? That's as good as saying, leave us alone. But suppose he were setting us up for something without letting us know?'

'Like telling porkies? He wouldn't do that, would he?'

Ash laughed. 'Can a robot tell the difference between a lie and the truth?'

Craig raised a finger. 'Why not? He's part human

isn't he – the molecular bit?'

'He's part biological, part electronic. That doesn't make him human. The point is why should he say one thing – no more tests – and do another?'

'Perhaps he's playing some game as well,' said Craig. He frowned. 'Dodgy game if it is.'

'Maybe – look, he's self-programming, but suppose his programme were altered? From Zarnia.'

Craig stared. 'That *is* dodgy. But what do we do?' He stopped. 'He could be listening in now. Maybe we shouldn't be talking about it.'

'Stop thinking about it, you mean,' smiled Ash. 'Not so easy.'

'Some — game,' said Craig.

'There's one way we can find out.'

'Which way?'

'Quite simple. Get him to help crack this Rachel business. If he won't then he is up to something.'

'And if he is?'

'Quite simple. Let's assume he's listening in, OK?'

'With you.'

'Now you and I make a decision. If Rachel's in trouble and has to leave Highwood, then we go, too.'

'You mean, pull the plug on his experiment?'

'Yes.'

'You're on. We won't let 'em mess Rachel about.' Craig rubbed his chin. 'There's a problem. How do we get through to Spencer? The bracelet's not working.'

'We don't get through. We pay Spencer a personal call.'

Ash faced downriver.

'Come on, a short walk to Heron Island.'

Chapter Sixteen

Kate was left to stew for the rest of the day. Miss Barker said no more but sent her to the changing rooms, then to eat.

She waited to be summoned to the Head, but no call came. So she stayed in her room, reading and listening to tapes. There was no sign of Rachel. Down on the river, thought Kate, rather guilty about shopping me to Barker or furious with me. Or both. Couldn't be helped.

By tea time the story was round the school: Falkon had been skinny-dipping with the Clayford rough trade and been caught at it. As she entered the dining room all talk stopped. Then a ripple of giggling spread round the hall. Someone shouted 'Oi, oi!' and every table burst into ironic applause. Kate gave a queenly wave of her hand and sat down.

Only two did not join in. Adrienne was tight-lipped and silent. Kate could see the wheels going round – was this good or bad for little Addie? Could she use the situation? And Rachel, at the other end of the table, sitting between two other girls, pretending to talk about the orienteering. She hadn't kept a place for Kate and didn't even look at her.

Half-way through the evening the word came. She went downstairs and into the Head's study. By now it was dark outside, but only the desk lamp was on. Kate could see Ms Hardy behind the desk and Miss Barker a little to one side. Kate giggled to herself, they're going to shine the lamp in my face.

The Head did not invite her to sit down.

'Kate, just tell me what happened – from your point of view.'

Kate did not pause for thought. She always did best on the run.

'I was off course, lost. I wandered round then found myself on the river bank. I could see the school from there. So I stopped worrying. But I was so hot I couldn't resist going in for a swim. Then Miss Barker came.'

'And the boys?'

'What boys?'

'Kate!' The Head's change of tone made Kate jump. 'Miss Barker saw three of you, quite plainly.

'You were reported lost by the river and Miss Barker went down to find you. She saw three bathers, one of whom was you. So, please Kate, no more fiction.'

Kate swallowed: 'There were two others.'

'Who?'

Kate did not answer.

'Kate. I shall not be pursuing these others, who-ever they may be. There is no need to do the *Mafia omerta* thing with me. I just need to know what is going on. I am responsible for you to your parents.'

Kate cleared her throat. 'We were just bathing.'

'I don't doubt that. But would you like to have your family in the headlines again – Falkon girl in nude bathing scandal?'

Without thinking, Kate said: 'If there's a story in the *Sketch*, we'll know who phoned it in.'

The Head tapped the table.

'Kate, this is no joke. Eventually I feel we shall have the Press down on us, with a great deal of unwelcome publicity.'

She opened the drawer in front of her and held up a white envelope.

'It's all here, isn't it? A well set-out case for your parents to take you away from the school. Only needs the date changing. I could save us all a great deal of trouble by getting rid of you. Then by the time the Press gets on to us you will no longer be here – end of story.'

Kate's throat tightened.

'Offer me a plausible reason for not sending this letter. Just one.'

Kate found her voice, in a rush. 'You won't believe this, but I had this idea for something sensational to wind up the concert programme – I mean end it. I was discussing it with these people –'

'By the side of your swimming pool.'

'That was something else. That was just a giggle.'

'A giggle?'

'But the other *was* serious. I was discussing this special act with them . . . really good.'

'Kate. I'm sorry, I do not believe you.'

Kate stopped talking. Silence fell. Outside it was quite dark. Miss Barker was almost invisible in the gloom outside the lamplight. Only the Head, face severe, was outlined in its glare. In the background a clock ticked the seconds away. As the Head eyed Kate, the darkness and silence seemed to deepen. Kate's brain worked, but no new thoughts came.

Then she jumped as the phone rang. The Head's

expression did not change as she reached for the receiver.

'Highwood School. I beg your pardon? Mr Boswell? I'm afraid I don't . . . Oh, I see. About the concert. Miss Falkon asked you to ring. Just one moment.'

Placing one hand over the phone, the Head gestured to Kate. Her lips formed two words. Kate leapt for the door and was out of the room in an instant.

Chapter Seventeen

The footbridge over the lock shook as Ash trotted over.

'Go easy. He'll hear us coming,' puffed Craig, trying to keep up with his friend.

Ash paused and looked back. 'Number One, SP12 is not a he or a she, remember? Number Two, Spencer must know we're coming anyway, and doesn't need to hear us.'

'Creepy,' said Craig.

'Not really – just we are not used to the way robots work.'

'Suit yourself.' Craig caught up with Ash and together they pushed their way up the narrow path overhung with bushes and ferns. 'No one would know there was anything up here. It's invisible except from the air.'

'Even from there,' said Ash mysteriously.

He pushed his way through the last of the under-growth and stepped out into the open.

'Lovely morning, Spencer,' he called. He turned to Craig who was close behind. 'See what I mean?'

The clearing was deserted. Apart from the old shed and workbench, there was nothing to be seen but grass and tufts of daisies and dandelion.

'He's cleared out. He was gone all the time. Didn't even say goodbye.' Craig sounded annoyed and relieved at the same time.

'Not gone. Just vanished.'

'Same difference.'

'Oh no. Spencer's here, somewhere, pretending not to be.'

Craig struck his head. 'Right. Camouflage! Let's see.'

He looked round then strode towards a low moss-covered bank and kicked it vigorously.

'Hell!' He hopped away clutching his foot.

Ash laughed. 'There's your capsule.'

'OK. So where's Tinny?' said Craig. He raised his voice. 'Come in SP12, your time is up.'

'Spencer's here,' Ash grinned. 'I'm sure.'

'Yeah. But not coming out. So what do we do?'

'Simple,' replied Ash. He moved to the workbench, bent over it and made rapid lifting movements, his hands slipping inside his jacket.

'What are you doing?' demanded Craig.

'Just nicking some of Spencer's gear. Come on.'

As they turned to go they heard the familiar voice from the doorway of the shed:

'It is not necessary to remove the equipment.'

While the boys watched, the grey metal capsule came into view as the green camouflage cover melted away. Rows of tools materialised on the workbench. Then Spencer walked slowly across the clearing.

Craig stifled a laugh. The robot was inside his 'human' form, but without clothes, minus the head and with the chest cavity open to show the metal inner body.

'You look obscene, Spencer, all nude,' he said.

'Do not understand the word. The clothes and the head-piece, while useful, are a hindrance in my work at the moment.'

He stood by the bench. The spectrum panel was flashing green to yellow. There was a touch of concern to the robot's manner, thought Ash.

'What do you wish? Why have you come?'

'I think you know, Spencer,' Ash answered in a serious tone. 'We need your help.'

'Explain.'

Ash shrugged. 'OK.' Briefly he ran through the happenings at Highwood.

'Why do you think I can help you?'

'We know you can help us. But, if you don't, Rachel may be forced to leave the school and the Valley. If she goes, we go too.'

The spectrum flickered to orange.

'That – is not acceptable.'

'I thought you'd say that. What will you do?'

There was the slightest pause, while the colours ran back through yellow and green to blue. Then Spencer spoke:

'I will help you. What do you wish to do?'

Ash explained while Spencer's rainbow colours switched rapidly to and fro. Finally he spoke. 'That is not easy. We shall need help. But it must be done with maximum security.'

'Leave that to us.'

Now Ash turned to Craig.

'Right. Let's go and see Bozzie.'

'Bozzie?'

'That's what I said.'

'Wait,' said Spencer. 'This person must not know about me.'

Ash laughed. 'When we've finished with you, no-one will know you!'

Chapter Eighteen

Highwood School Hall was crowded. Parents stood in small groups, stiff and embarrassed, some silent, pretending to study the pictures on the wall or the decorations, some talking too loudly. Teachers and girls moved to and fro with cups of tea, plates of sandwiches and cakes. Family Week had begun.

Kate, busy with last-minute preparations for the concert, looked out from behind the curtain drawn across the platform which now acted as stage, and smiled to herself. This was going to be an evening to remember in the Falkon career. It would either be a triumph or a disaster with everything slipping into a deep hole in the middle of the floor.

It all depended on Bozzie and the boys who had promised to deliver a special item to crown the concert. They had their own reasons for helping, which made Kate a trifle nervous, but she refused to think about them.

She realised that in recent weeks she had become very skilled at controlling her mind. Ideas no longer flooded in and out at random. If she didn't wish to think along certain lines, she didn't. If she wished to work over an idea, then she could concentrate her mind on it like a spotlight. It made her feel good and she needed that because beneath the surface, panic was never far away. Things could go very badly wrong with her life if she lost control.

Her glance took in Adrienne. This wasn't difficult.

The little porker was everywhere, trolling from group to group with Daddy in tow. If Mrs Dyott existed, she was not on display, but Daddy was. Mr Dyott, thought Kate, was not like his daughter. Tall, with an impressive bald polished head and rimless bi-focals behind which a very sharp pair of eyes looked out. Only that nose, short, broad, with wide nostrils, was like his daughter's. So alike that Kate had to stifle a laugh.

Maybe that was why, when she first caught sight of him she had the feeling they had met before. But that was absurd. It must be the nose. She had been fooled by that familiar snout. It must run in the family. Kate giggled.

From her vantage point, she noticed Rachel standing in a corner of the hall.

Rachel had barely spoken to her for days now, only the few words needed when they were together in their room. That hurt, yet Kate knew it was partly her fault and that she could do nothing about it. She just had to grit her teeth and trust things would work out. Some day soon, she told herself, everything would be all right again. Right now, she must busy herself with the concert.

Then she noticed the old white-haired couple with Rachel. They looked lost. The old man, thin and bent; the woman, short, sharp-featured. This must be Gran and Grandad.

Impulsively Kate leapt from the platform. She must go and speak to them. This place must be a total embarrassment for the old couple. But as she pushed her way through the crowd, her arm was gripped. She saw Adrienne's pink face.

81

'Oh, Kate, I've been looking everywhere for you.'
The voice rose sharply, making heads turn – as was
intended, thought Kate grimly.

'You must meet Daddy. Daddy, this is Kate
Falkon. You know Piers and Helen, of course.
Daddy knows everyone in show business.'

The rimless glasses turned on Kate. There was a
thin polite smile as she was shrewdly sized up. She
gazed back, not willing to be intimidated and again
she had the feeling she had met him before. It must
be the nose.

He was speaking: 'I don't think Kate's parents
will see themselves as show business, Adrienne,
dear.' The voice was quiet, level, but supercilious.
There was an edge to it that told Kate this was not
a man to cross.

Adrienne turned pink. 'Well, they are, sort of.
They're so often on the box.' She rattled on, trying
to stop me talking, guessed Kate. 'They'll soon be
here for the Wildlife Convention, of course we're all
wishing they might have time to come down to the
school, but I suppose they'll be too busy. You know
what it's like, Daddy.'

Kate drew away. She felt Dyott wanted to talk
to her, but that did not suit her. She moved on
to Rachel and her grandparents. But Addie was
following her, squealing:

'Oh, here's another friend, Daddy, Rachel. She
lost her parents, poor thing. These are her grandparents.' The voice seemed to have a giggle in it.
'He's a lock-keeper. Isn't that thrilling?' She made
it sound ridiculous, thought Kate.

Kate saw the old man flush. She felt, rather than

saw, Rachel's fury. She could not meet her friend's eye but tried quickly to think of something that would separate her from Adrienne in their eyes.

Then to her surprise, several of the parents nearby turned and formed a ring round Rachel and her grandparents. One man, spluttering in his eagerness, thrust out a hand saying,

'I say, which lock?'

The old man's face was a study.

'Claremont.'

'You don't say. Did you hear that, dear? We sometimes come through. Though I don't remember actually meeting you.'

Kate saw the old eyes suddenly alight with amusement at some past incident. 'Oh yes – I remember, last July. The *Lucky Strike*.'

There was a sudden hush. Then a woman spoke.

'You can settle a little dispute –' she looked round coyly, '– a bet actually, between my husband and me. Just how deep are the locks on the Clode?' Kate caught a flicker in Rachel's eye. Typical, using the old name for the river. 'I say it's four foot eight, he says it's five foot.'

As the old man answered, Kate saw the expression in Rachel's eyes had changed. She was smiling now. Adrienne was already steaming away from the group, and Kate moved too. It would be curtain up very soon.

The concert was ending. It had all gone well, barring normal accidents. The balcony from which Adrienne was trilling, 'Romeo, Romeo, wherefore art thou Romeo?' had threatened to collapse at one point. But, to Kate's chagrin it had held up and Adrienne, pinkly proud, had come back twice to the stage to take her bow.

Half the choir had sung a different chorus from the other half, but the audience had pretended not to notice and rushed to applaud.

She began to think that all might go well. But she knew that the real testing time was to come.

She sent a quick glance through the tall windows which overlooked the broad sweep of gravel in front of the school. The boys had promised faithfully they would arrive on the dot of 8.30. Now it was 8.27.

She sprang up the steps on to the platform.

'Now, ladies and gentlemen. My pleasure, our pleasure to offer you a very special, totally original entertainment to crown our Family Week Concert.'

The gravel drive was still empty. She gritted her teeth.

'So original is this act by –' she paused, '– friends of Highwood, that even I do not know what it is, but rest assured it will be – sensational.'

As she spoke, the audience had turned to the scene outside. There came a series of bangings and grindings as if a tortured engine was giving up the ghost.

Girls started to giggle. It spread to the parents. Even the staff forgot to shush and joined in. People pointed. Smaller girls rushed to the window.

Kate closed her eyes then forced them open.

An ancient van, battered by many a knock on the road, thick with grease and dust, puffed and wheezed up the drive. Across the front of the van was strung a crude banner with the words: *Bones and Co*.

The engine gave a final devastating bang, the bonnet jerked and the truck halted as the audience exploded into uncontrollable laughter.

Chapter Nineteen

As the sound of laughter, shouts of 'Any old iron,' and 'Rag and bone,' swelled, Kate raised her hand to call for order, but spotted Adrienne in the front row and stopped. Two pairs of eyes were on her, one malicious, the other speculative. She dropped her hand and waited for the noise to die down.

It stopped suddenly. An expectant silence took its place as the door of the van was thrown open and three evening-suited figures stepped out to stand in line by the bonnet as if awaiting a word of command.

One was broad-shouldered, dark-haired and wickedly handsome. That must be Bozzie thought Kate, admiringly. And she was not the only one.

'Ooh, dishy,' whispered a voice. Chuckles competed now with shushing noises – from the parents this time.

'No, I prefer the tall brown one. He looks a mystery man.'

'No, I'll have the little one. He's cuddly.' Kate grinned. If Craig could hear that.

Bozzie waved his hand. The three marched to the rear of the truck. An astonished gasp came from the hall as they heaved into view a full-sized coffin with gleaming brass handles. Raising it to their shoulders, they began a slow march towards the school main door.

Kate felt her elbow touched. Miss Hardy was

behind her. 'I hope this is is not going to be –
inappropriate, Kate.'

'No way,' said Kate with a confidence she did
not really feel. They wouldn't do anything to upset
people, would they?

The tall doors swung open and the procession
moved up the hall, watched in silence. The closeness
of the coffin and the solemnity of the bearers silenced
the gigglers. The adults were silent out of politeness,
curiosity and perhaps apprehension.

The three mounted the platform, and placed the
coffin not flat but standing on its end. Bozzie nodded
grandly to Kate and turned to the audience.

'My lords, ladies and gentlemen.' He leaned forward and lowered his voice. 'I know you're all as
common as muck, but I'm taking no chances. Let
me introduce my team.

'I begin with myself, Boswell, known to my friends
as El Magnifico. My friend Ashok, named after the
great Emperor, as you all know of course; a master
of the prestidigitation of the East. And last but not
least, the Demon Bike Rider, Craig, who has been
persuaded not to do his flaming hoop act tonight,
but instead to help with special effects.'

He paused for a polite round of applause then
raised his hand again.

'I shall begin with . . .'

At this moment there came a loud echoing knock
from the coffin. The hall froze into silence. Bozzie
turned irritably.

'Just cut that out, Bones. You can arise later
on.' He turned back to the audience. 'If we let
Bones out it'll stop the show. Bones has been in

there three hundred years and can wait another half hour.'

Nervous laughter died away. Craig brought a card table to the middle of the stage and Bozzie began his tricks. Slowly the audience fell under the spell of some of the oldest pieces of magic, like the pea and thimbles. One after another came up from the audience, trying in vain to beat Bozzie and his flickering fingers and distracting patter.

Ash played tricks with scarves and cards, Craig moved swiftly to and fro with the props. The clapping grew louder and more frequent and Kate began to relax.

But there was still a note of excitement and tension in the air. Half the audience still had their eyes on the upright coffin.

And at each quiet moment the hall would suddenly resound with hollow knocking. No matter how often it happened it reduced the audience to nervous silence.

Bozzie would bellow, 'Shut up, Bones. You'll get out later.'

The girls picked up the phrase, shrieking 'Shut up, Bones,' then relapsing into tense silence. If that coffin wasn't opened soon, thought Kate . . .

At that moment, every light in the hall went out. With a creaking, grinding sound, the coffin door opened.

In the dark opening appeared a tall skeleton, bones picked out with a phosphorescent glow.

'My lords, ladies and gentlemen,' chanted Bozzie, 'I give you Bones in his first public appearance since 1693. *Then* he expired. Tonight he is inspired. Bones.'

Nervous squeals were followed by dead silence. Then one bold spirit began to clap.

'Dem Bones, Dem Bones, Dem Dry Bones –'

But the song stopped abruptly as the skeleton began to speak in a light, level voice.

'Thank you, thank you. I am happy to be with you today, all one hundred and thirty-seven of you, one hundred and five females, thirty-two males, with an average age of twenty-nine years, seven months and sixteen days.'

'All right Bones, stop showing off,' said Bozzie. 'As you see, Bones has not been wasting time. Bones knows everything. Everything, you say? We'll put it to the test. Ask any question you like.'

A small girl put up her hand.

'Are you a boy or a girl?'

'What do you wish to know for?' replied Bones. 'At my age it is irrelevant. I am neither a him nor a shim.'

'Oh, Spencer,' thought Kate. 'You're giving the game away.'

'What's seven hundred and sixty-nine times eight hundred and forty-three?'

'Six hundred and forty-eight thousand, two hundred and sixty-seven,' came the instant answer, 'but why bother me with such trivialities?'

Now the questions began to come rapidly from the floor: history, geography, current affairs. It was like some crazy master-mind programme, thought Kate. Bones neither hesitated nor faltered. The answers flowed as freely as the questions. Sometimes Bones excelled and the answer nearly came before the question.

Now the skeleton mocked the audience.

'Trivial, irrelevant matters. Any computer of the most primitive kind could answer them. Let us have something to test my mind.'

Taken aback, the audience fell silent. What are you up to, thought Kate. Bozzie stepped forward.

'Well, if there are no more questions, and it is already nine-thirty and the parents ought to be tucked up in bed with a cup of hot cocoa, I will –'

He was interrupted by a voice from the floor. It could only be Adrienne, Kate knew.

'If Bones is so clever, can he or she tell who is the ghost of Highwood, and who is stealing our belongings?'

Ms Hardy spoke from the front row. 'I'm not sure that is a suitable question, Mr Boswell.'

Bozzie answered grandly, 'Ms Hardy, you may rely on Bones, who reached the age of discretion two centuries ago.'

Then Bones cut in, 'A difficult question, but one I shall enjoy answerering.'

Now the silence in the hall was absolute. Bones waited as if to raise the tension higher, then spoke:

'There is no ghost, naturally. Ghosts are immaterial therefore illogical, serve no purpose, have no survival value, are contrary to every principle of science and exist only in over-excited imaginations *or* –' the voice paused, '– as a form of diversion to cover unacceptable activities . . .

'As to the thefts of trivial objects, a pen, a small blue earring, a handkerchief with the letter "S" embroidered on it and so on and so on, these are *not* the work of a ghost.'

Another pause.

'But they are not the work of the person who has been accused of them. They are the work of someone else trying to divert attention from another theft which has not yet taken place but which will happen inevitably.

'The person asking the question has an interest in this matter, knows more than they have said, but less than they would like ... The objects in question are all to be found under one of the chairs in the common room.'

The lights came on. Several girls were on their feet, but Ms Hardy waved them down.

'Please stay where you are. Miss Barker will kindly check if the – answer – is correct. Perhaps, Mr Boswell, you can complete the act.'

The lights went out. Bozzie called:

'One final question before we bury Bones again.'

A man's voice from the front of the hall: 'I have a question, one we would all like answered.'

Someone stood near the stage. Kate guessed it must be Mr Dyott. The voice was controlled but brittle. Something had got under his skin.

'How do you people, from outside the school, know so much about its affairs? Leaving aside your party tricks with a computer and a skeleton you can only have had this information from someone inside the school. If so, we ought to be told who is revealing this information about the private lives of our daughters.'

A rush of hand clapping stopped as Bones replied: 'Firstly, I am not a computer in the sense you mean it – the sort on which you store your information about other people's private lives. Secondly, no one from the school has assisted me. Thirdly, I could not reveal any of my sources if I had such.'

'Why not?' There was indignation in the voice, but Kate felt it was put on.

'For the same reason that you will not reveal the sources of your information about your – subjects. You, sir, know more about some persons than they know about themselves. Who do you choose to reveal your secrets to?'

Now Dyott had really been stung.

'I am a biographer – of well-known people. My information is revealed only in my books . . .'

He paused as if to control his voice, then went on, 'We are entitled to know what is behind this masquerade.'

The hall lights went on as Dyott sprang up the steps to the platform, evaded Bozzie's outstretched arm, pushed Craig to one side and seized Bones with both hands.

Next moment there was an echoing *bang*! as the coffin door slammed shut. Dyott stagged back and fell to the floor clutching the skeleton in his arms. As he landed the bones separated and showered around him.

Bozzie, quick as light, sprang down to help Dyott to his feet, turned to the audience and bellowed, 'Thank you Mr Dyott, sir, for helping us to bring our performance to such a dramatic conclusion.'

Grabbing Dyott's hand, he held it aloft while the audience burst into applause.

Adrienne's father recovered himself, bowed to the audience. His daughter turned to her neighbours and said in a high-pitched voice, 'Of course, Daddy was in on the act all the time. But he never said a word. So clever.'

Miss Barker came back into the hall holding up the vanished objects. The Head swiftly mounted the platform.

'Thank you Mr Boswell, thank you Ash, and Craig. Thank you for a – most original and even thrilling act, which I hope will help to put a stop to our mystery at Highwood. Thank you, everyone who made the evening a success, and now I wish you all a very good night.'

As the hall emptied Bozzie and the boys, followed by a stream of girls, were bearing the coffin from the hall. Dyott, face inscrutable, Adrienne hanging on his arm, was shaking hands with the Head.

Suddenly Kate remembered where she had seen Dyott before. It came to her in a flash. And in a flash she tried to suppress the thought. But she was a fraction of a second too late. She had thought the thought and now must face the consequences.

Chapter Twenty

'You were totally brilliant, Spencer,' Rachel told the robot. The four of them sat on the grass in the clearing on Heron Island. Spencer, perched on the work bench, did not answer but the colours on his spectrum panel shifted towards the warmer range.

'He's modestly pleased with himself,' thought Kate trying to work out just what was going on in that Zarnian brain. Spencer had astonished her by the performance at the concert and almost thrown her off guard. Not the way he had answered all the questions, or even revealing where the stolen objects were, but the way he had provoked Dyott. Why? Spencer had been 'persuaded' by the lads to go to Highwood to take the heat off Rachel. But why stir it up for Adrienne's Dad?

Deep in her mind she suspected why, but checked her thoughts from venturing down that channel immediately. Aloud she spoke flippantly.

'You were the greatest, Tin Thing. But I wish you'd wear your head when you're off duty. It's off-putting.'

'Spencer's lovely, however,' said Rachel. 'Besides, if the head's on, which personality do we get?'

'Right,' put in Ash. 'When the head's on it's usually someone else, not the Spencer we know and love.'

'I can adopt a neutral personality, an entirely artificial one,' said Spencer. 'Like this.'

The robot took the plastic headpiece with its light brown hair from the workbench and raised it to the shoulders of the dummy body. Kate grinned as she remembered the crazy day when Ash and Craig had taken it from the skip outside the clothes shop and careered through Clayford, with those thugs Stevens and Rodder, then the police, after them.

From that day on, Spencer the machine, had started to seem like one of them. Perhaps it was a good idea to recall that this was a robot, and an alien one at that.

The head clicked into place and like a film the curved blank face began to fill with an image that grew more real as the features took shape.

'I want Captain Picard,' said Kate; 'no hair.'

'Why not Madonna?' said Craig sarcastically.

'No, that's just right,' said Rachel as the face settled down to a handsome boy/girl image.

'Too wimpish,' jeered Craig.

Spencer strengthened the jawline. Craig snorted with laughter.

'Oh, butch.'

'That'll do,' put in Ash, 'Spencer'll have an identity crisis. Seriously,' he went on, 'you were great last night. Bones was terrific.'

'Yeah,' added Kate, 'now the heat's off Rachel, we can relax.'

This was no less than the truth, she thought. After the concert Rachel had slept soundly. This morning her cheeks were bright again. The pallor had gone. She threw back her hair and laughed.

'Right on,' Craig said. 'Now I can get back to

some serious biking instead of poncing about like an undertaker.'

'Waiter,' grinned Ash. The dark suits for the concert had been borrowed from his father's colleagues at the Taj restaurant.

'The point is, Rachel's off the hook, but who *was* stealing the gear?'

Craig shrugged. 'What does it matter? Probably that little cow Adrienne. Whatever, whoever, it won't happen again.'

'Right,' added Kate quickly. 'No more trouble from the adder, so we can forget the whole thing.'

'Hold on,' said Rachel. 'My troubles are over, but what about yours?'

'Mine?'

'Don't be so annoying, Kate. You know what I mean – your parents, those stories in the Press. There are bound to be more by the time they arrive in England.'

Kate laughed and lay back on the grass.

'My parents ignore the tabloids, like they ignore anything that doesn't interest them. They couldn't care less about what the world thinks.'

'I believe you,' Craig agreed. 'If you're famous you have to take the good publicity with the bad. It's all rubbish, anyway. See the garbage they write about biking.'

'Wait,' said Ash, 'this is more serious than that, isn't it? This rag has got hold of stuff about Highwood and Kate. Her parents stuck her in there to get rid of her – more interested in animals than their own daughter. That's dirt.'

'Right,' added Rachel. 'And how did they get

the connection? It must have been Adrienne and her father.'

'But Dyott's not a journalist, he's a biographer, nothing to do with wildlife – well, the animal bit,' said Craig grinning. 'He got really wound up about that at the concert.'

'Huh,' snorted Rachel. 'He's like his daughter. Tell any lie if it suited him.'

'Thing is,' Ash said thoughtfully, 'we know what motive Adrienne has – to get even. What's his motive? What's the link there? I don't think he'd do this just to please her.'

'No, that's crazy,' Craig agreed, 'there'd have to be something more. Like big money. I mean what would he get for giving tips to a rag like the *Sketch*? Not much.'

'Whatever it is, it's a rotten thing to do to people like Kate's mother and father,' said Rachel angrily. 'What have they done to deserve it?'

Kate lay face to the sun, eyes closed, and spoke lightly. 'When you've all done fretting about my family. Listen, the *Sketch* never mentioned my name, nor Highwood. They may not even know. It'll all blow over. In ten days' time Piers and Helen, eco-stars, will be here and gone again. As Craig says – you want to be famous, you have to take the dirt as well.'

'Kate, how can you talk like that about your parents?' Rachel's voice wavered. 'If it were mine, I couldn't bear it.'

Kate eased herself up, looked round and said coolly, 'Well, it isn't. It's my parents, so that's the end of that. Now, unless you have anything more important to talk about than Piers and Helen Falkon, I'm off.'

With that she stood, strode off through the bushes and vanished, leaving the others staring at one another.

Craig got up. 'Me too. I'm off to get my bike.'

'Just a minute, Craig,' Rachel spoke warmly. 'You can't just clear off like that. This is serious. We have to do something.'

'Like what?'

Rachel swallowed. 'Like finding out if Adrienne is passing this stuff to the papers and stopping it before Kate's parents get here. If we don't it'll do a lot of harm to them, to the school, to Kate herself.'

Ash nodded. 'Yeah. I wonder if she really feels like that, as though she couldn't care what happens?'

Craig looked at them both.

'You know, you two can't understand what it's like to have parents and not have them at the same time. I know just how Kate feels.'

'Maybe,' Rachel answered. 'That doesn't make it right. Slugs like Adrienne shouldn't be allowed to spread their poison.'

'So what are you going to do?'

'We could keep an eye on her. See where she goes – what she does.'

'Tap her phone?' asked Craig ironically.

'That's not so stupid,' said Ash. He turned to the robot. 'Could you do that, Spencer? Find out what Adrienne is up to?'

'It is possible –' began the robot.

'Great!' Rachel's voice was eager.

'But I will not.'

'Why not?' demanded Ash and Rachel at once.

'Because Kate does not wish it. It is her – concern.'

'But you did – at the concert.'

'That was because you requested help for Rachel. She wanted help. I am permitted to intervene in such cases. But not where Kate refuses.'

Ash brooded over this a moment then said, 'You know, Spencer – I've often thought about you and your game rules. But what is the game? I mean, what is this Experiment all about?'

The spectrum panel moved towards orange red as the robot's human face dissolved. Then as quickly the colours died and the face returned. Spencer was smiling.

'When the time is right, I shall be permitted to answer your question. You will be told all. Now it is not possible.'

'OK. But why have *you* been sent? Why not a human – a bio? I mean a Zarnian bio. Why send a robot to make contact on its own with bios down here? I mean, you said robots are robots, humans are humans. They have different rules.'

Spencer spoke firmly, almost intoning: 'Robots are a crucial feature of Zarnian life. The aim of robots is to make life better. Robot evolution is specific. Bio evolution is random, takes millions of years to cause essential changes. Robot generations follow swiftly on one another and their evolution is controlled. Change can be made at will, within the limits of technology.

'Robots are also – expendable. They are sent on distant missions so that bios shall not be put at risk.'

'But bios would do the job better,' argued Ash. 'You are the greatest, Spencer, but you admitted that even our feeble brains are thousands of times more complex than yours.'

'More complex, more interesting, but less predictable and less reliable. And slower.' Spencer paused. 'So robots serve bios. According to rules.'

Ash grinned: 'Right, but you're a self-programming robot, SP12. You're a bit like us. You make decisions. You do unexpected things, like the way you needled Dyott in that concert.'

'That was – an error. I was playing a role. I allowed myself to explore the limits of that role. I overstepped them.'

'Role?' asked Ash. 'You can play roles? Can you tell lies, Spencer?'

'I do not understand the question.' There was a finality about the robot's tone.

'You don't choose to,' Ash began, then stopped.

Rachel spoke quickly: 'I understand Spencer, but you'd help Kate if she really needed it?'

'If she really wished it,' the robot corrected.

'Or if the needs of the Experiment required it,' put in Ash suddenly.

'I cannot discuss the Experiment,' the robot answered.

'Ash, give it a rest,' interrupted Craig. 'I don't know if you can wind a robot up, but you are seriously trying.'

'Sorry, I was role-playing. Got carried away.'

'You will be, if you don't knock it off. Listen, Rachel,' Craig went on. 'I think tailing Adrienne is stupid, pointless. You can't really want to do it.'

Rachel answered calmly, 'Yes, I do. I don't think Kate really knows what's best. She's just thinking how she feels herself. So yes, I do want to go on.' She paused. There was a gleam in her eye. 'I want to get my own back on Adrienne – is that enough reason?'

Craig laughed. 'That'll do for starters. But don't let's do anything stupid. OK?'

'OK,' said Rachel gratefully.

'Right, I'm off,' grinned Craig. 'Will you come and tune that engine for me, Ash?'

'If I can't get any more out of SP12. We'd better go.'

As the three left the clearing, Spencer slowly removed the headpiece and moved across to the capsule by the shed wall.

Chapter Twenty-One

Initiator to	SP12: Report received and acknowledged. The situation is interesting. But time is short. When do the girl Kate's parents arrive?
SP12	In seven Earth days.
Initiator	Her alienation from them is growing. You must take steps to make this complete. Her detachment is vital to the success of the experiment.
SP12	Acknowledge: If we move too quickly then we shall lose her.
Initiator	That is your task. Detach her from them and retain contact with her.
SP12	That may not be possible.
Initiator	I am not expressing an opinion. I am giving an instruction.
SP12	My ultimate task is to preserve all contacts for the Experiment.
Initiator	I designed this Experiment. I decide what your tasks are – ultimate or otherwise.
SP12	Acknowledge.
Initiator	You are becoming too closely involved with these personalities. You show signs of developing loyalty to individuals rather than commitment to task. The eco-neural element in you is to make your technical functioning more flexible; it should have no emotional content.

SP12   Acknowledge.
Initiator   A word of warning. You may play Guess
            One, Guess Two, Guess Three, with your
            contacts. Do not attempt to play this
            game with me.
SP12   Acknowledge.

Chapter Twenty-Two

Rachel's call came at the wrong moment for Craig. He was at the foot of the basement steps about to open the door to the recess where his bike was stored.

It had once been a coal store, fed from the pavement above. But he had swept it clean of coal dust and whitewashed the walls. Now it housed his bike, gleaming silver and blue. Ash had tuned the engine to concert pitch. It was a fine Saturday morning and he was just about to go down to the Hollow.

He felt the familiar tingling at his wrist and swore. The bracelet was clouding. But this time there was no rainbow tinge. Spencer seemed to have ironed out that little fault.

Rachel's face appeared, eyes sparkling.

'All ready, Craig?' came her silent question.

'Yeah. But we may be talking about two different things. What's going?'

'Haven't you read the *Sketch* today?'

Craig snorted. 'Read a rag that doesn't know a Yam from a Teasmade? No I don't and I haven't.'

'It's another load of dirt about Kate's people.'

'Tell me something new.'

Her thought voice was serious now. 'There *is* something new. I'll read it for you. One of those caption stories:

'Piers and Helen Falkon, homeward bound – if England is home to a couple who've clocked up more hours in the jungle than Tarzan. Due in London any day now for a cosy chat about crêches and other caring institutions among the apes with their fellow wildlife freaks.

'And, so we hear, a not-so-cosy chat with the Head of the very exclusive school where they parked their little daughter. It is said a letter will soon wing its way Africa-wards asking the celebrated couple to take their little brat back to the chimps before she disrupts the ivy-covered halls any more.

'Or maybe the letter's being kept for them. Either way the letter is there . . .

'What exactly does it say? That'd be telling. Watch this space.'

Craig frowned. 'That is dirt. This is that stupid letter Kate faked up when she arrived, isn't it? How have they got hold of it?'

'Maybe they haven't. If it had been taken, Kate would have been told. But they know about it. That means only one thing.'

'Like what?'

'Adrienne is the only one who knows about that letter.'

'So?' Craig was wary.

'Well, you agreed to help keep an eye on her.'

'Sort of.'

'Listen. Adrienne's made a phone call and now she's set off for town. She left ten minutes ago and she should be half-way there. You can pick up the trail as she comes over the bridge.'

'Look, Ray. I'm about to go down the Valley. Can't you get Ash to follow her?'

'I asked him. He says you'd be – less conspicuous.'

'Do me a favour.'

'Craig, please. She'll soon be in Clayford. We need to know why. What's she up to?'

'Probably shopping.'

'Maybe, but supposing . . .'

Craig gritted his teeth. 'OK, but this had better be worth it.'

'It will be.'

Craig saw Adrienne as she came off Bridge Road and round the corner into the High Street. He was inside the bike shop pretending to look through a mag, when he saw her cross the road heading towards him.

As he watched her Craig reluctantly agreed this was no shopping expedition. Adrienne walked quickly. Her face was flushed, her eyes set. She was excited.

Just in time, Craig remembered to lift the mag in front of his face as she reached the pavement. For a second they were a few feet apart, separated by the window. Then she moved off down the High Street.

Tailing her was easier than expected. She looked round only once, as she crossed the road. Craig dodged into a shop doorway. He lost sight of her, swore and leapt across the road amid hooting traffic. Just in time her saw her back as she turned into the McDonald's.

He paused by the window, face hidden by the menu card. Adrienne, inside, was heading for a table in the corner, where a man was sitting. It was Dyott. This was important, Craig knew.

'Daddy!' he heard Adrienne's voice.

There was no welcome, just a curt nod that made Adrienne sit down and keep quiet.

Craig, eyes on the couple, sidled into the eating place and bought a coffee at the counter. It took all his spare cash. Did you get expenses on this caper? he wondered sourly.

Coffee in hand, he moved sideways. They were deep in conversation, heads bent. He needed a table where he could watch without being seen. The best place was gone, though, occupied by a young man, his back to Craig, who seemed to be fiddling with his Walkman. Craig quietly took a place on the other side, back to Adrienne. He could hear at least from there.

Their voices were low, the father's almost a whisper, Adrienne's more high-pitched.

'I don't understand it Daddy. Kate doesn't seem to be bothered – that story in today's *Sketch*. But Rachel's furious. If looks could kill.'

'What does she know?'

'Nothing. I expect she's guessing. I know what's in that letter, but I haven't seen it since I handed it over to the Head like a good girl. Guessing I'm the source is one thing; proving it's another.'

Father was unimpressed. His reply was cutting.

'Pity you didn't think of copying that letter at the time.'

'But Daddy,' she wailed. 'How did I know it mattered – like that?'

'Well, you know now. What about Miss Falkon?'

'That's the incredible thing. She's sort of – blithe.

Walks about whistling. Says "Hello, Adrienne darling" and things like that.'

Dyott nodded. 'Perhaps she really does want to land her loving parents in it.'

'Ooh, maybe. What next, Daddy? It's really exciting.'

'Keep your voice down. We need the letter. The *Sketch* has been after me for it. They want proof. These stories are libel without it.'

'What do you mean – Daddy?' Adrienne's voice was smaller.

'You've got to get that letter. It ought to be easy. That place has no internal security. You told me – confidence policy.'

'What if I get caught?'

'You won't. Now all that excitement's over nobody'll be about at night. Take you five minutes at the outside. It'll be worth it – for more than one reason.'

'Don't worry, Daddy, if I can fix her, I'll be over the moon. But, there's one thing I don't understand. You don't normally deal with the Press. You call them awful names. And the *Sketch*! I mean. What's in it for you?'

'You mind your own business, Adrienne. You just do what you're asked and keep your nose out of everything else.'

There was a scrape of chairs being pushed back. Dyott passed so close to Craig, he brushed his sleeve. Craig lowered his head as Adrienne went out. At the door she turned. It seemed their eyes met.

Craig ducked so violently he knocked his half empty cup over. The coffee ran down his jeans. Swearing to himself, he bent below the table level.

When he raised his head, she was gone.

Chapter Twenty-Three

The Head looked at Kate across her desk. The *Sketch* was spread out between them. She nodded.

'I saw it yesterday.' She shrugged.

'You take it very calmly,' said Ms Hardy.

'What can I do? Burst into tears?' Kate saw the Head's expression change and hurried on. 'I mean, there's nothing I can do. It's typical Press rubbish. It means nothing. They haven't got the school's name and they haven't even got the letter.'

'Those details are being saved up for maximum impact when your parents land at the airport. As to the letter, I'm afraid they may indeed have it – now.'

'*What*?' Kate was half out of her seat, then sat down. 'I'm sorry. That was rude. But it seems only a day or two since you took the letter out and showed me.'

'I specifically looked for it yesterday – after this.' The Head tapped the newspaper. 'It was still there. This morning I happened to look again. It was gone.'

'That's it then,' Kate said.

'That is all?'

Kate forced herself to sound more serious.

'If anyone should be asked about this letter it's Adrienne. She knew it was there. She knew what was in that letter. Oh, yes, she did. Whatever she told you when she dutifully handed it over, she looked inside. She could probably quote it verbatim, but she needs the evidence to get her money.'

'Money?'

'Adrienne's not in this for the good of the nation.'

'I'd be better pleased, Kate, if you would stop pretending this is a huge joke.' The Head tapped the desk. 'I have already asked Adrienne. She denies taking the letter. She asked for her room to be searched. She was quite calm and – genuine about it.

'She told me that she has known about the letter from the start. If she really hated you she could have harmed you before now. Now she says that's all over. She quite admires you, even if she doesn't like you. Why should she do such a thing now?'

'Pretty good,' murmured Kate ruefully.

'She said something more. She admitted she was up last night. She couldn't sleep. In the passage just by this door she saw Rachel. And Rachel pretended to be sleepwalking.'

Oh. What was Rachel up to now? Kate could have sworn her friend hadn't stirred last night. Still, she wasn't awake all the time and Rachel was bent on proving Adrienne was up to her tricks – obsessed with it.

'I don't know,' she told the Head. 'I thought Rachel had got out of the sleepwalking bit. I just don't believe Adrienne.'

'That is your choice, Kate. As far as the disappearance of the letter goes, I am inclined to accept her word. But the question remains, what to do if the letter is published and the school named. What about the school, what about yourself?'

Kate thought a moment.

'Can I speak straight?' she asked.

'When did you do anything else, Kate?'

'I honestly don't think this business matters. The school can't suffer. All the story says is that you deal with difficult daughters of wealthy parents here. You do. Like Adrienne, like me. You do a great job.'

'But the letter is a forgery, Kate.'

'I know, and if it ever comes out the forger will confess and be cast into outer darkness. It will be one more example of the sort of thing Highwood copes with.'

'You are serious, Kate. You don't care if we have to – let you go?'

Kate looked at the Head, thinking carefully before she answered.

'Why should I? The alternative is for my parents to take me back with them to Africa. I never wanted to leave.'

'Or send you to another private school?'

'I'd run away. I'd cause a real scandal and I'd give the *Sketch* exclusive rights. I'm not being funny, Ms Hardy. I'm not showing off and I'm not trying to wind you up.'

'I'm sure of that, Kate. But your parents. Do they deserve this? Are you so furious with them you don't care what happens?'

Kate stood up, her hand on the chair back.

'As my parents told me when they left me here, they're old enough to manage on their own now.'

Chapter Twenty-Four

The Four stood on the bridge looking downriver. Rachel had called them to an urgent meeting. There had been a fierce, inconclusive argument and now they were silent.

At last Rachel spoke, frustration making her voice break slightly.

'There must be *something* we can do tomorrow. Your parents are flying into trouble at the airport. Can't we at least warn them?'

Kate shrugged. 'The Head tried already. But no contact. That's how they operate. They'll work up to the last minute, tear through the bush like maniacs in their Land Rover. Freshen up at a hotel for an hour, then on the plane looking suave and elegant. Forget it, Rachel, there's nothing you can do to help them.'

'But they've no idea what's waiting for them – Dyott and that letter, the whole load of filth.'

'Rachel, love, my parents are so used to the media they won't even blink. Nothing upsets them.'

Ash shook his head. 'Kate, I think you're mistaken. This story is going to make them look silly at the Convention.'

'How so?'

'Oh, Kate. They'll be giving talks about family structure, protection of the young, care and all that. And the Press – all of it – will be poking fun at them, the family experts great on chimps, pity about the humans. It makes them look small and that's the idea.'

'Well, is it true or isn't it?'

Rachel suddenly blazed at her friend. 'To hear you talk, anybody'd think you were desperately neglected and unhappy. You're OK.'

Kate was about to reply, when Craig spoke.

'How do *you* know how anybody feels – just 'cause they cope? You do cope, without your parents, or with one parent. What else do you do? Jump in the river?

'No, you live life the best way you can. If there's any fun going, you grab a piece. And then people say – look how well they're coping, doesn't seem to have done them any harm. It must be a whole month since they threw a fit and foamed at the mouth. We can all stop worrying.'

Rachel was silent. Ash turned from looking downriver.

'All right, all right. Don't let *us* fall out. I think the way Kate looks at things is strange, but I can try and understand it. Let's imagine for a minute you know Kate's parents but you don't know Kate. What would you do, Rachel?'

'I'll tell you what I'm *going* to do. Tomorrow at 10.30 I shall be catching the bus at the bus station. When I get to the airport I'll try and see them before the Press do. And I'll tell them. I'll do anything I can to stop Adrienne's little plot.'

'That's a bit of a liberty,' said Kate ironically.

Ash smiled, shook his head. 'You said your parents are on their own. That's as far as you're concerned. Fair enough. But can you give me any reason why one shouldn't stop someone else

113

– whoever – being made a fool of by rubbish like this?'

He turned to Rachel.

'I'll be with you tomorrow. It's a slim chance. But I'll give it a try.'

'Count me out,' said Craig. 'I agree with Kate. Let it go.'

He looked at Rachel's face and lightly punched her shoulder.

'I know we Four stick together as a rule. But we can't just think alike all the time.' He paused in sudden thought. 'I don't suppose Tinny'll help after all?'

Rachel shook her head. 'No, no contact. I rowed up to Heron Island, first thing. He wasn't there.'

'Hiding,' said Ash.

'No. I searched the place. He's vanished.'

The bus station café was crowded but Ash found a table by the window. The two of them had arrived early – Ash out of habit, Rachel out of anxiety.

'Sit down,' he said soothingly. 'You have to relax, Ray. That plane won't be in till noon. There'll be lots of waiting around. Get you a drink, eh?'

She nodded gratefully. When Ash had gone she took a paper from her pocket. She had written down all that she wanted to tell the Falkons when they arrived. When she started this task last night, the whole story sounded incredibly long and complicated – and unbelievable. She'd torn the pages up and concentrated on the main things. She knew there would be very little time and she must convince them. They mustn't think she was crazy.

'Why, it's Rachel. Fancy you being here.'

Adrienne, in a pale blue outfit, made up, stood by the table. There was a smile on her face, like a cat with cream on its whiskers. Rachel stared back. Adrienne laughed.

'Please yourself. I'm off to the airport – meeting Daddy. We're joining the Press in the VIP lounge. I don't mind telling you now, because it's all over bar the shouting – and there'll be lots of that.'

She turned and rolled her eyes at Ash.

'Oh, hello. The gang all here. Well, well. Oh no, that rather bad-tempered little ginger boy won't be coming. That's a relief. But don't tell me Kate's giving it a miss. Mind you I don't blame her. It won't be pleasant for her or her parents.'

She looked at the two of them as if something had dawned on her.

'Don't imagine you can do anything about it. You need a pass to get into the VIP lounge. So don't try. Don't do anything silly. It won't work. Unless dear Kate can fix things for you. She usually does.'

'Who's taking my name in vain?'

All three turned. Kate, smartly turned out in an outfit Rachel had never seen before, stood there, travelling bag in hand. She smiled provokingly at Adrienne, who had gone very quiet. At last she spoke.

'Even if you do turn up, it won't make any difference,' she said at last. 'It'll just be more embarrassing.'

'Darling Adrienne,' said Kate. 'Why should I spoil your big day? I've just come to see off Ash and Rachel. If they want to go autograph hunting, good luck to them. You won't catch me wasting my time. Go on Addie, enjoy it as much as you can.'

She turned to Rachel.

'Rachel. Can I convince you? You'll only upset yourself. You too, Ash. I think you're doing this just to be nice to Rachel. It's very admirable, but there's no point. Addie's right. You won't get into the VIP lounge. When you're dealing with slick operators like the Dyotts, experienced dustbin dippers, you don't stand a chance. But suit yourselves. See you for tea, eh?'

She lifted a hand and walked away across the crowded cafeteria. Outside, Rachel saw her pause to chat to a man in uniform. She smiled at him, then laughed, looked at her watch, nodded and walked to the exit.

Rachel gritted her teeth and turned back to Adrienne.

'You'll be finished at Highwood after this.'

Adrienne smirked. 'Don't upset yourself. My bags are packed. After this I can pick any school and Daddy'll take me there. Today I shall really enjoy myself.

'Oh, look, the bus is in . . .'

Chapter Twenty-Five

Craig sat on the pavement outside his home and cleaned the bike carefully. He was ready to take it down to the Hollow. Bit stupid, cleaning it, in a way. There'd been rain the night before and the bike would be plastered in mud by the time he finished.

But he liked to start clean. 'Championship style every time,' his Dad had always said. He stood up and flung the rag he was holding savagely down the basement well. Why did he have to think about his Dad, now?

He rocked the bike forward, swung it round and made ready to walk it down the slope towards the tunnel under the railway. But he didn't start the engine here – that just got up people's noses. And you never knew when someone might tell the Law.

It must have been yesterday's argument about Kate and her parents that made him think about his vanished father. If only he could be as cool as Kate, letting Ash and Rachel go off to the airport just like that. Still, she was right, there was no point. She was tough, was Kate, hard even. But she made sense. That was the way life went. Why pretend people were decent and you should do your best?

'Craig.'

He turned and almost let the bike fall.

Kate stood there, dressed up and made up. He'd never seen her like this. She looked older – and very expensive.

'Hello,' he said, baffled.

'Craig. Will you do something for me?'

'Like what?' He was wary.

'Give me a lift across the valley, to the bypass over the other side of the country park?'

'Take you?' He nodded at the bike. 'These aren't made for two.'

'Let me ride it, then.'

'Forget that.'

'Anyway, it'll take two. Spencer toughened the frame, I know. He said it'll last longer than you.'

'Why can't you go by bus, or take a taxi?'

'Because I don't want anyone to see me, and the bloke who's picking me up shouldn't be doing it.'

'You can walk.'

'Like this? No, it'll take too long. Craig, listen – I don't want to offend you. But I know you're short of – cash. To join the club, all the gear. I'll pay you what you need if you'll do it for me.'

He laughed, sharply. 'Stuff it, Kate. You must be desperate if you'd say a thing like that.'

'I *am* desperate.'

He looked her over. 'You can't ride like that. There's mud in the valley.'

She grinned as if she'd won him over. She opened her bag, took out a light overall, put her smart jacket into the bag, then pulled on the suit, and zipped it up. Sliding her arms through the handles of the bag, she looked at Craig and grinned.

'Ready when you are.'

It was a crazy ride, across the scrubland, swerving

118

to and fro around bushes and brick mounds, bumping over rocks and ruts in the path. Twice on the greasy ground they skidded, the back wheel slewed round and Kate fell, smearing her overalls. She got up, painfully, and limped to the machine. But she made no complaint, took her place again and they set off.

On the towpath Craig let rip, jerking his head round now and then to watch for the water bailiff, flipping neatly aside to avoid anglers with their large green umbrellas and spread of gear.

At the Heron Island lock, Kate slipped down while Craig wheeled across. The next hundred yards was a nightmare, crashing through bushes, slashed at by thorns, wheels spinning.

Suddenly the old mill sprang into view against the green and white of the marshes.

'Jesus,' yelled Craig. 'There's a hole in the bridge. Hang on.'

She felt the machine ride air, then the jarring thump up her spine as they landed.

Now the going was easier, bushes spread out, grassy slopes. Craig skirted the park, eyes guiltily peeled for wardens. How was he going to explain this if they caught him? He didn't even know what Lady Kate was up to.

At last they scrambled up a slope and stood on the hard shoulder of the bypass. Kate stiffly climbed off the bike and stared up the long vista of highway shimmering with heat haze.

'I think that's my lift coming. Goodbye and thanks a million, Craig.'

He grinned. 'Never say goodbye. I'm coming with.

You won't tell me what you're up to. I want to know. You owe me. This is payment.'

She glared at him defiantly for a few seconds then laughed.

'You win.'

Chapter Twenty-Six

Passengers swarmed from the coach, grabbing luggage, rushing to the check-in points as if their lives were at risk. Adrienne, smiling to herself, stepped daintily through the glass sliding doors and set off across the concourse. Every now and then she half turned as if to see whether Rachel and Ash were following. At each turn her smile broadened.

The VIP lounge was down an unmarked side passage and this was already crowded with people who all seemed to know each other. They shuffled feet, called first names, made jokes and gave sly looks at the TV camera men as they dragged their gear into the room beyond. At the door an airport official was checking passes. The crowd moved in slowly, good-humouredly, as if the day was before them and it was going to be entertaining. Ash stretched up to see into the room beyond – rows of chairs, the glare of powerful white light.

Ahead of them Adrienne was stopped at the door.

'Only Press, Miss.' The official was polite but amused.

'I think you'll find my father is in there, Roger Dyott.' Rachel heard the voice, pitched a little too high, and suddenly had an idea of how Adrienne would be in ten years' time – someone used to dealing with doormen.

The official was impressed. He signalled to someone and a moment later, Adrienne vanished into the crowded room. She allowed herself a last backward glance; as if to say, 'So long, suckers,' thought Ash.

Now they were at the entrance. The noise and heat from the room hit them.

'Sir?' the man at the door addressed Ash. He seemed not to see Rachel.

'We need to speak to Mr and Mrs Falkon.' Ash couldn't use first names like that.

The man grinned openly. 'So do sixty other people. Question is, do you have an invite –' he paused ironically, '– or do you know someone inside?'

Ash was no good at lies. The humiliation of being found out was enough. He hesitated.

'It's very important. We need to speak to them before they meet the Press.'

'No way. Even if I wanted to I couldn't help you. The drill is, they come off the plane and straight into the lounge. Even I won't get to talk to them. Sorry – sir,' the tone was friendly, but final.

'Let me write a note.'

'Sorry. It's not on. After autographs?' he asked sympathetically. 'Give me your paper and I'll ask them if I can after the press conference.'

Rachel lost patience.

'It's about their daughter, Kate. She's a friend of ours.'

He was impressed by the urgency in her voice.

'Really? Now if she were here, we might do business.'

'We're not sure where she is . . .' Rachel's voice faltered.

'I see.' The man became brisk. 'Look, there are

people waiting patiently behind you. Can you move to one side, please?'

Ash and Rachel looked at one another hopelessly. They turned to go. From inside the packed lounge, they had a last glimpse of Adrienne's flushed, triumphant face.

They walked back to the concourse, Ash slowly, Rachel still hurrying.

'There's just a chance,' she gasped. 'If we could get out on the runway, we might catch them as they leave the plane.'

'No, Rachel,' Ash was sharp, 'there's no way we can even get out. The security's too tight. I'm afraid there's no more we can do.'

But Rachel was not listening. Half turning, she pointed and screamed:

'Look – look who's there!'

Hurrying up an escalator came a smartly dressed girl, followed by a smaller boy in mud-spattered jeans and jacket. They set off at a run towards the far end of the concourse.

Ash called, 'Kate, Craig, what's going on?'

Either they did not hear or were not listening. The speed at which they ran set Ash and Rachel into motion. They followed at a furious pace, dodging groups of travellers, trolleys, cleaners with trucks.

Cutting across, Ash, now breathless, caught up with Kate. She stared blankly at him.

'What's going on?' he demanded. Kate ignored him. But Craig, breathless himself, simply pointed.

Ahead of them and just visible through the cross-movements of the crowd a figure was moving purposefully, not running but going at a tremendous rate. Next moment, it had vanished round a corner.

'Come on!' Kate suddenly spoke and the four followed, round the corner, down one passage, into another, each one darker, more deserted than the last. Now there was their quarry just ahead, pausing by a small door.

A quiet buzzing and the door swung open. The figure passed through, the door swung back. But not before Kate was there, foot thrust into the narrowing space. The others piled in behind her.

Now they were in a long ante-room with chairs. Kate put a finger to her lips. They went forward quietly now. But the figure ahead did not turn. Instead, it stopped at a further door. Again the buzzing sound. Again the door was opened but cautiously, inch by inch.

Beyond was noise, light, warmth, people. Again Kate signalled for silence. One by one they followed her through and the door closed again. They were in the VIP lounge.

Chapter Twenty-Seven

At first the noise and glare confused them but Kate did not hesitate. She began to circle the room, now jammed with men and women. All the seats were taken and the space behind was full of standing people. Some turned and looked curiously at the four as they stole along the walls. But most were too busy with what was going on in front.

Kate edged forward and now Ash could see where she was aiming for. Behind the TV cameras and the metal struts of the arc lamps, the tangle of cables and bustling men in jeans and sweaters, was an empty space, near a door. From there he guessed, they could see what was going on, while the lamps' dazzle would conceal them from any interested eyes.

They had barely reached their vantage point, pressed uncomfortably together, when someone called from the front:

'Can we have the door closed now? Nearly time to start.' Outside sounds were cut off and the crowded room slowly became quiet.

At the front an elegantly dressed publicity officer with a sheaf of papers was tapping a microphone. It gave a light howl. She grimaced and the audience chuckled. She smiled and spoke.

'Good morning, everyone. Well, good afternoon, by exactly one minute. Our guests today, Piers and Helen Falkon, need no introduction. Which is just as well because we do not have unlimited time. The flight has landed – early – and is disembarking. They will be with us in just ten minutes – someone else is seeing to their luggage,' she added ironically.

'They sent word they will answer questions – provided the questioners are identified – for half an hour.'

There was a shout of protest. She raised a hand. 'Maybe we can stretch that a little. How many definitely, I mean seriously, have questions?' She stared at the hands and said, 'All right, all right. I'll try and get them to make it three quarters of an hour. But, I did warn you. Now, if you can bear with us for another five or so minutes . . .'

A voice cut through the chatter. 'Can we have that set on at the front? "Regional Round" is covering – while we wait.'

There was a laugh. Heads turned. Kate nudged Ash. 'Pound to a penny that's Adrienne's Daddy.'

The large television set was switched on. The screen cleared to a studio, a newscaster, a fixed smile, then the picture changed to another ironic burst of applause as the VIP lounge came into view. The newscaster was saying in the background: '. . . waiting for Piers and Helen Falkon, world wildlife mega-stars, in England on one of their very rare visits.'

The image changed. Rachel gasped. Ash put a finger to his lips. On the screen was Dyott talking to a reporter with hand mike. This is going over live, thought Ash.

'Mr Dyott, you've made a special study of the Falkons during your distinguished career as a bio-grapher. How long is it since we saw them over here?'

Dyott smiled. 'Oh, five, six years at least. To be honest, they see Africa and the Zarambete Rain Forest as home. England is where they come to attend conferences, when they feel there is something they absolutely must reveal to their fellow scientists.'

'They are regarded as top in their field?'

Dyott's smile grew thin. 'Once unchallenged. Now there is competition, a new generation of researchers. They have, after all, been at their work for twenty years now – mature people . . .' He paused. 'They have a daughter of thirteen . . .'

The reporter had his cue: 'And where is she – in Africa with them?'

Dyott's smile became a smirk.

'That is supposed to be confidential. Let's say she is in a very special private school not a million miles from here.'

'Ah, what is so special about the school?' Now the reporter was smirking. It was catching, thought Ash.

'Put it this way. For people who have children who are pretty brilliant, but developing so rapidly that they are –' he paused delicately, '– a bit of a handful, and are too busy to cope, then the particular school is, I believe, ideal.'

'Ah, yes,' fed in the reporter. 'The Falkons are renowned for their studies of family life?'

'Among animals,' swiftly put in Dyott.

'Among animals,' agreed the reporter.

Suddenly the screen went blank. There was a buzz of talk, a few hand claps. The lady's voice was heard calling, sharp and commanding.

'Set's on the blink. Can we have it attended to?'

As she spoke a young man appeared behind the set, bending down, pushing buttons, testing cables. There was a sharp click and the screen lit again.

'Not very clear, is it?' grumbled someone.

The screen brightened. The reporter had gone but Dyott was still there. He came into sharper focus, and seemed to be amid a small crowd. Rachel gasped, grabbed Kate's hand and squeezed it.

A background voice was speaking, quietly but distinctly. Dyott held a tea cup. His lips moved but no sound came out. The camera shifted angle slightly and Adrienne's face appeared, unmistakeable. The voice-over went on:

'Mr Dyott, of course, knows what he is talking about. His daughter Adrienne attends the special school in question, along with Kate Falkon. Adrienne –' her face suddenly filled the screen,' – is something of a handful herself, but has her uses. She is the source of most of the gossip about the Falkons and their daughter.'

The silence in the press room could be cut with a knife. The voice-over went on, 'This is grist to the mill for Dyott.'

Adrienne and her father were now seen in a café, heads bent, whispering together. Craig turned and punched Ash, silently pointing.

'Here we see Dyott persuading his daughter to steal a letter from the school, allegedly asking the Falkons to remove their daughter . . .'

A close up of Adrienne, then,

'. . . Adrienne does not like the idea, but her father is rather insistent. He has his standards as a researcher – relying only on primary sources.

128

He has his standards, too, about the obtaining of evidence. But with the Falkons, against whom he has old and painful scores to settle, then methods are no object.'

Someone gasped from the audience: 'That is libellous, but libellous. What is the Beeb playing at?'

Another voice gave a strangled shout, 'That's not the BBC, that's a video . . .'

Lights went out. From brilliant glare the room dived into complete blackness. The television image vanished. From beneath it came a sudden click, a crash. A second later the lights were on, the television working again. The picture cleared. There were Piers and Helen Falkon walking down the plane gangway.

From the front came the lady's voice again.

'Sorry about that. Totally baffling. Let's switch the set off anyway. We'll have the real thing in –'

As she spoke, the door opened and Piers and Helen, in immaculate safari suits, entered to a sudden, surprised round of applause.

At first the questioning was slow and almost awkward. The quality newspaper journalists asked high-level questions about the Falkons' forest project.

They answered crisply and good humouredly, more than once adding, 'The full story we shall keep for the Convention. I'm sure we shall see you all there.' That won a quick laugh.

Then the tabloid reporters moved in.

'We've heard a lot about your daughter and her schooling. Just been watching a fascinating little film about it.' The laughter rose, and fell. 'How do you feel? Quite happy?'

There was a moment's silence. Piers frowned but Helen spoke calmly.

'It doesn't seem fair to talk about our daughter in her absence. She is at an excellent school, Highwood, which I recommend to any of you. I'm sure she's happy there, but when we see her later today, I expect we shall get a full report.

'Without betraying confidences I can tell you that Kate is not the sort of person who will put up with unacceptable conditions without saying anything.' She smiled. 'She's like her parents.'

'Ah,' pursued the journalist, 'the question is, can people put up with her?'

Piers was half on his feet, but Helen rested a hand on his arm and he sat down again. The questioner continued.

'We've heard about a letter from Highwood asking you to remove your daughter from the school. What truth is there in that?'

There was a silence as the Falkons looked at each other. They had gone slightly pale. Rachel felt her stomach grow cold. This was the awful moment. What would Dyott do? So far there had not been a word from him.

Someone spoke from a corner.

'I can explain about the letter.'

Heads turned. Kate was pushing her way through the crowd. Her parents, thought Craig, are totally gobsmacked. If she wanted to put them through the wringer, now was the time.

Kate turned to face the audience.

130

'I know all about the letter. I wrote it. It's a forgery. The Head said it was so good it almost fooled her. It was,' Kate looked down, 'my idea of a joke, a very private joke. I had no idea that anyone would want to steal it. But sadly there are people who will try and do things like that for reasons of personal spite and –' She paused for a moment, then raised her voice, '– worse still, you people make your living out of this; people's problems, people's ill-will. You have a go at personalities in public life.

'You find fault with them. You write articles and editorials about them. But the methods some of you use are just the pits. You tut-tut in public and in private you say, "that was a bloody good story."

'My own regret about this is that this stupid joke gave some people a chance to get at my parents. We can all have family rows.' She paused again. 'How many of you ever quarrel with your daughter? And how many of you invite the neighbours in when you do?'

Kate suddenly stopped as if regretting her impulse. The room was in uproar. Camera flashes filled the air like a storm. The Falkons were on their feet now. And the commanding lady's voice was heard above the racket:

'I honestly think we've had that question answered. Unless you'd like Kate Falkon to tell you all off a bit more.'

The Press Conference was over, the room emptied. The journalists had left, some in a hurry to reach offices and phones. A small group tried to find

Dyott and Adrienne. But they had mysteriously disappeared.

Ash, Craig and Rachel, dazed but relieved, watched Kate chatting to her parents.

Then an airport official bustled up. 'Did any of you by any chance see that young bloke who fixed up the television? He wasn't one of ours. I'd like to have a word with him.'

'Bloke?' said Craig. 'What bloke?'

Chapter Twenty-Eight

Kate forgave her parents – almost.

They certainly impressed her.

When the Convention was over, and the talking and lecturing and arguing were done, they did not depart like other people for a round of trips to zoo or lab, to receptions and parties.

Instead they came quietly down to Clayford. They visited Highwood School and made themselves agreeable. Then, without Kate reminding them, they went on for an assembly at Valley School.

Loaded with flowers and chocolates they called in on Ash's family, had tea with Craig and his mother – easily, modestly.

They called in at Claremont Lock to see the old couple and got Rachel to lead them round the secret places of the Valley for a whole day.

Discreetly they made presents to Ash and Craig. They had done their homework, chosen the right things. Kate knew when her friends were pleased, and they were.

Last of all they told Rachel that when the operations were over, she should come out to Zarambete to rest and then to work. 'You are a born biologist,' Helen Falkon told the stunned girl. She meant it, Kate knew; and she was right.

It was a perfect three days when nothing went wrong and all that was wrong from the past seemed to be put on one side and forgotten.

Kate was ready to forgive her parents – nearly.

What threw her off balance was what happened after the Press Conference as the car drove away from the airport.

Her father turned to her and said, 'Kate. We talked it over. You were right, we were wrong. We miss you very much. We want you to fly back to Africa with us.'

Chapter Twenty-Nine

As the roar of the Falkons' departing plane died away overhead, the Four sat at a window table in the lounge. There was a relaxed but expectant air about them. No one seemed to want to break the silence.

At last Ash spoke:

'All right, Kate. Tell us. Just what has been going on? For weeks you kidded us you couldn't care less about your parents. Then you stage that last-minute drama at the Press Conference.'

'You and Spencer,' added Craig. 'So, what goes on?'

Kate looked round at the other three and grinned in an embarrassed way.

'OK, OK. I'll talk. But promise there'll be no comeback.'

'Get on with it,' urged Craig.

Kate was serious now.

'First of all, I have to grovel to Rachel. She got the thin end. And the worst was, I couldn't tell her. I had to appear to believe she was going round the twist.'

Rachel's eyes widened.

'Why had to? You could have told me. Why play that game?'

'That's it,' said Kate. 'It was a game. I've been playing this game, with Spencer.'

'Ah,' murmured Ash, as though something was beginning to make sense. 'But what game?'

'That's the crazy thing. I don't even know, but it felt like bluff, double bluff, treble bluff sometimes.'

'I *knew* Spencer was up to something,' Ash said. 'That rainbow tinge on the bracelets. Not getting through to you, him being out of contact. But how did you know?'

'I was lucky at first. When things started to go missing, I thought it was Adrienne, trying to stir it up.

'But I realised it wasn't her, though she was being opportunist, making use of the thefts. Still, there is no way she could have even known about the magazine with the story on my parents. Someone else took it from my room, ringed the item in red and put it in the common room.

'Who knew? Only Rachel. The funny thing was that I believed it was her for long enough to fool Spencer.' She put a hand on Rachel's. 'That was the worst about it. I did actually think it was you.

'Then the bracelets playing up made me think again. It couldn't have been Rachel, but it must be someone else, someone with a long term plan, to get me to –'

'To what?' asked Ash eagerly.

'Wait a bit . . . to decide once and for all where I stood with my parents . . . That was what it was all about, and the other thefts were just a blind. And that was the really dodgy moment.'

'How?' Now all three spoke at once.

'Because I was aware somewhere deep inside my mind that Spencer was probing my thoughts all the time. But it must have been at a level Spencer couldn't reach . . .'

'So?'

'So, I had to know what was going on, what the next move in the game might be, like playing chess over the phone or blindfold. I knew I had to let Spencer think one thing while I was getting behind his guard.'

'But how could you do it?' asked Rachel.

'That's the weird thing. Because I half believed it was Rachel stealing, because I was really angry with my parents, because I was actually *capable* of hurting them, I could let Spencer think that was all there was in my mind.'

Ash nodded. 'A robot might not be able to guess how two-faced a human being can be.'

'Three-faced,' went on Kate. 'The thing is, when I understood what the game was, I stopped trying to protect myself and began to play for real . . .'

'I pretended so well Spencer had to do something about Rachel. I could have taken the heat off her before that, but then Spencer would have known I'd sussed him out and tried something else which might have fooled me. I needed to know just exactly what he was up to. So I had to play stupid games with Rachel.'

'And with us,' said Craig. 'You fooled me. I was on your side. I was gobsmacked when you did that U-turn in the VIP lounge.'

'Oh, Craig,' said Rachel. 'Would *you* really go the whole way and humiliate your parents –'

'Come on,' interrupted Ash. 'That's not a fair question. And it's Kate's story.'

Kate nodded. 'I know Craig's feelings. He's pulled every which way, like I've been. It isn't a question

137

you can say "yes" or "no" to. But I was grateful to Craig for backing me up at the time. It helped me in the game and –' she paused, '– it helped me to feel normal at a time when I didn't know what was really me and what was the player in the game.'

Ash suddenly banged the table.

'You threw Spencer completely off balance. At the concert, he started on at Dyott. I couldn't make that out. Why had he been probing Dyott? He must have hacked into Dyott's pc. Dyott nearly went spare.'

'Yes,' answered Kate, 'but I think that was deliberate. It was Spencer's most brilliant move.'

'How?'

'Yes, he said himself he'd overdone the role he was playing.'

Kate nodded. 'Well, sometimes the most brilliant chess moves come on the spur of the moment. Even the mover doesn't know what's going to happen.'

'And what did?'

'The craziest thing. I suddenly looked at Dyott's face when he fell off the platform clutching Bones. He was livid, his features all screwed up, like a stroppy kid. I knew where I'd seen him before. Years ago when I was about eight, we were in a hotel. It could have been abroad, it could have been in London. I think it was London. It's all vague.

'I wanted something and I rushed into my parents' room. They were there with this man. He was staring at them and his face was twisted with rage.

'I could heard my father speaking. He could be so cutting and contemptuous. When Dyott fell off the stage those exact words came back to me.

'"Your approach, Mr Dyott, might do for actors

or pop stars or people who bother about public opinion. But for serious people, for people with real work to do, it is worse than useless, it is positively poisonous."'

She shook her head in amazement.

'I didn't understand what he was saying, though I knew Dyott was humiliated at being told off. I didn't understand the words, but I remembered them . . . and when I did I knew why Dyott and Adrienne were trying to stir it up. Dyott wanted revenge.

'But in that second when I remembered I tried to get rid of the thought, so that Spencer wouldn't know. But it was too late. I knew Spencer would swap tactics, so I had to do the same. What would really put Spencer on the spot?'

'If your parents took you back to Africa,' blurted out Ash.

'Who's telling this?' retorted Kate. 'I played that line for all it was worth. That was easy, because it was true. It was the last thing I wanted, but I could think it. What I had to do was convince Spencer I didn't care.'

'So?' All three leaned forward.

'So Spencer and I were both on the same tack, though he didn't know it. He was bound to try and cock up what Dyott was doing. I had no idea what he could or would do, but I knew somehow he would find a way of totally silencing Dyott – and he did.'

'That's it!' said Craig so loudly that heads turned at the nearby tables. 'That young bloke in the café. I thought he was fixing his walkman. It was Spencer, filming Adrienne and her Dad. Crafty sod.'

'The video was fantastic,' put in Ash, 'so smoothly

done, they all thought it was part of "Regional Round".'

'Except Dyott,' said Kate, 'he knew what it was but it was devastating, particularly that bit about old scores. It silenced him totally and put most of the Press on my parents' side.

'I almost felt sorry for him and Addie. You see after that kerfuffle, no other school wants to know about her.'

'So, what will they do?' asked Rachel.

'Don't worry. She's coming back to Highwood. Daddy crawled to Ms Hardy. Ms Hardy agreed. But one false move from dear Adder and she is out on her wriggly tail.'

'And that letter?' demanded Craig.

'That was brilliant. Ms Hardy found it back in her drawer next day. She's almost convinced she mislaid it and it was never taken.'

'What a wizard Spencer is.'

'Kate was pretty fantastic.'

Kate shook her head.

'No, I was half way there in my mind all the time. I was never completely lying. That's why I was convincing. When my father told me in the car they wanted to take me back to Africa, I nearly passed out.'

'Why?'

'Because I didn't want to go but I wanted him to say it. When I'd got him to do what I wanted I no longer wanted it. After all the bluff and double bluff of the last few weeks, it was too much.'

'So what did you say?'

'First I said, "Let me think about it". Later I told him I'd come out for a while with Rachel . . .'

She looked at the others.

'You see, I've really got to be independent now. Being stroppy is easy, and childish. I realised, when I was pretending, just how irrational it was. I think my parents and I understand one another now. We need each other, we know it. But – I nearly blew it.'

'It was so risky,' said Rachel. 'But what was it all about? Why did Spencer do it? He'd agreed there'd be no more tests. Why did he lie like this?'

'Lie and lie,' answered Kate. 'I've thought about it off and on and my best guess is he was made to. He got new instructions. He had to carry them out. But he was trying to let us know. That rainbow tinge on the bracelets, that looked like a fault. I'm sure it was on purpose. He was playing a fantastic game of bluff, bluffing us and – maybe bluffing someone else. That's why he stayed away.'

'But why, why?' Rachel was baffled.

'I think,' said Ash, 'I'm beginning to see what this Experiment is about. We've always believed it's about testing us for some reason. But suppose it were just to test Spencer . . .'

'How?'

'Well, for example: how far can you push an eco-neural, self-programming robot in the direction of being human – before it ceases to be reliable as a robot . . . ?'

'Starts being stroppy?' said Craig.

'Starts having doubts?' went on Ash, his face serious. 'The point is we have to realise what this means for us.'

'For us?'

'Yes. We can't just treat Spencer as one of us. We can't just rely on him. I think he wants to play it straight with us, but he's – he's vulnerable to pressures from . . .' Ash pointed vaguely into the air.

'Poor Spencer,' said Rachel.

Ash nodded. 'In a way, yeah. But don't forget the risks in all this, for us.'

'Oh, come on, Ash,' teased Kate. 'Don't you want to know where it's all leading?'

''Course he does,' said Craig. 'We all do. But we've got to watch out, find out more. Somehow we'll have to get to know what these Zarnians are after, why they need us. Right?'

'Right,' said the others.

Chapter Thirty

Initiator to RS349: Report on latest stage of Experiment received and analysed. Satisfactory.

RS349   Satisfactory? The girl was reconciled to her parents. The mission failed.

Initiator   You have, of course, no imagination, RS349, but should grasp logically the value of the test.

RS349   Do not understand.

Initiator   The girl's performance was brilliant. She was better than all my expectations. I have never known Guess One, Guess Two played more subtly and convincingly.

RS349   In the end SP12 did not carry out the instructions.

Initiator   SP12 was also brilliant. It is difficult from Zarnia to understand the unpredictable irrational Earth bio-behaviour. He is closer. In the end he took the right decisions.

RS349   He allowed the other contacts to know what was happening.

Initiator   Yes, that was unnecessary, and disturbing. He protected the Experiment by protecting the group. He followed instructions but also carried out his own programme.

RS349   That is not acceptable.

Initiator	Correct. So far his robotic and bio elements are in balance, but this is not a fixed state.
RS349	What if he should move too much on to the bio side? That could be fatal for the Experiment.
Initiator	It will be fatal for SP12 in that case.
RS349	So what are your instructions?
Initiator	We continue with the Experiment and see what happens.